"I don't k[now] what yo[u mean]"

Joanna struggled to keep her voice steady, still shaken that the fall she'd taken the night before had left her so helpless and vulnerable. "You could quite easily arrange to have me moved to town. It's obvious you're trying to keep me here."

"Quite." Hal clipped the word out. "You should rest here, where I can look after you."

"You're keeping me here against my will, and I won't stay."

"Very dramatic," he drawled. "But I doubt if you could drive in your present condition."

Her hands gripped the edge of the duvet. "*Why*, Hal? Why are you behaving like this when things are the way they are between us? I know you've got another girl. So why?"

"Let's just say that last night put ideas into my head," he said slowly. "Let's say I'd forgotten how good it was to be in bed with my wife."

MARJORIE LEWTY is a born romantic. "It's all in the way you look at the world," she suggests. "Maybe if I hadn't been lucky enough to find love myself—in my parents, my husband, my children—I might have viewed the world with cynicism." As it is, she writes about "what is surely the most important and exciting part of growing up, and that is falling in love." She and her family live in Leamington, a pleasant town full of beautiful parks and old Georgian homes.

Books by Marjorie Lewty

These books may be available at your local bookseller.

Don't miss any of our special offers. Write to us at the following address for information on our newest releases.

Harlequin Reader Service
901 Fuhrmann Blvd., P.O. Box 1397, Buffalo, NY 14240
Canadian address: P.O. Box 603,
Fort Erie, Ont. L2A 9Z9

MARJORIE LEWTY

villa in the sun

Harlequin Books

TORONTO • NEW YORK • LONDON
AMSTERDAM • PARIS • SYDNEY • HAMBURG
STOCKHOLM • ATHENS • TOKYO • MILAN

Harlequin Presents first edition November 1986
ISBN 0-373-10932-6

Original hardcover edition published in 1986
by Mills & Boon Limited

CHAPTER ONE

'Do I *have* to go, Richard? I suppose it's just silly and sentimental of me, but I'd much rather someone else went. What about Giles? The Riviera's his patch, isn't it, and as he's already down in Nice couldn't he go along to Menton and combine the Villa Favorita job with the hotel one?'

Joanna's clear, musical voice was steady but Richard Kilburn, proprietor of the prestigious firm Kilburn Europroperties Limited, and her employer for more than two years, had only to glance at the huge misty grey eyes that met his own across the desk in his London office, to see that she was alarmed. More than alarmed, Richard admitted to himself; under her usual poise the poor girl was petrified. Richard was well aware that Joanna Daley was much more sensitive than she cared to display to the world in general, and this particular assignment had to be a traumatic one for her.

But business was business. Richard pushed his large thick spectacles further up his nose and folded his plump hands on the desk and said regretfully, ' 'Fraid not. Giles has got as much as he can cope with on the hotel transfer. The new owners are putting in a lot of hi-tech equipment, he told me on the phone yesterday, and he's got himself involved in that—all part of the service, of course. And Don and his missus are still awaiting the arrival of their first—much overdue. It's more than my life's worth to suggest sending him out of the country just now.' He coughed. 'I can see the—er—difficulties in asking you to try and sell that particular property, Joanna dear, but as you know the place so well, and as the owners have asked for their personal property to be packed and shipped to them in Canada, it does seem that you're the best person for the job. I don't see Giles folding up frilly undies very nearly, do you?' He chuckled and Joanna smiled back obligingly, although she was not feeling at all like smiling.

'And this American bloke appears to be our best prospect to date,' Richard went on. 'If we don't sell soon, we'll have to fall back on the alternative of letting to tourists; that was something the owners suggested. They don't like the idea of the villa standing empty too long, particularly as they didn't have the opportunity to go down there and put things to rights before they had to leave for Canada. So that's the position, my dear, and as a personal favour to me—will you go? It'll be beautiful down there in May.'

'Oh, Richard, you old fox.' Joanna's laugh was unsteady. 'I suppose I'll have to, if you put it like that, but I must admit it's a job I don't exactly relish.' She smoothed back her dark hair with a hand that shook a little.

She stood up, straight and slender, and

Richard thought for the umpteenth time what a beautiful girl she was. She was immaculately, almost fastidiously turned out, in a charcoal suit with a silky blouse in a deep wine shade, echoing the colour of her carefully-tended nails. She was, Richard told himself with satisfaction, the very picture of a top professional young woman and he was very lucky to have her on his staff.

She sighed now and pulled a face at him, making a joke of something that was going to be painful for her—but that was Joanna all over, she never moaned about things that couldn't be changed. 'OK, Richard, if you're not going to let me off the hook I'd better go and see about booking my flight.'

Richard nodded. 'Good girl. Let me know times and I'll phone through to Giles in Nice and get him to meet your plane and arrange transport to Menton for you.' He thought for a moment. 'Maybe when you get through with La Favorita you could have a few days in Nice with Giles—he'd appreciate that, I'm sure.' He cast a sideways glance in her direction.

'That would be pleasant,' Joanna said composedly. 'I could give him some help with the paper-work perhaps. That hotel sale seems to be hanging on. It *is* going through OK, is it?'

'Oh, yes, fortunately, but it's a pretty big job.' Richard grinned. 'I expect he could use a bit of help, but that wasn't exactly what I was getting at.'

'No?' Joanna said innocently. She smiled into Richard Kilburn's plump face, and he knew she had guessed why he had suggested the mini-holiday for her with Giles—to make up for what would surely be, for her, a painful opening of old wounds. 'Don't worry, Richard, I won't go all nostalgic about La Favorita, it's all in a day's work. Oh, and by the way——' she turned, smiling, on her way to the door '——Giles and I are just good friends.'

'I felt like an ogre,' Richard admitted that evening to his wife, as he recounted the doings of the day, as usual. 'Sending Joanna down to Menton smacks too much of returning to the scene of the crime. I know she and her husband spent several holidays at the Villa Favorita before it was finally sold.'

Mary Kilburn heaped a second helping of her husband's favourite apple tart on to his plate and said placidly, 'Or you might say it would be like getting behind the wheel again after a car accident. Always the best thing to do. And anyway, it must be nearly three years since the break-up of Joanna's marriage, and I'm sure it wasn't her fault.'

'*She* walked out on *him*,' Richard reminded her. 'I remember that distinctly.'

'Well, he must have driven her to it.'

Her husband clucked his tongue. 'Women!'

'Well, what happened this morning? Did she agree to go?' Mary Kilburn was always interested in the doings of her husband's highly successful agency, which was based in London but specialised in selling luxury properties in European jet-set playgrounds.

And interested, too, in his staff; especially in Joanna Daley. Mary liked to think she had some understanding of young people, having brought up and married off three daughters of her own. But Joanna Daley was still a puzzle to her. Joanna, Mary thought, was one of the most beautiful girls that she had ever seen, generously including her own pretty daughters. The slender body and long, elegant legs; the sleek black hair framing a perfect oval face; the great grey eyes with their long curving lashes; the flawless skin faintly flushed with pink; the alluring mouth. It all added up to a breathtaking effect.

And yet—Mary had more than once seen those limpid grey eyes harden, that soft mouth draw itself into a straight line that seemed to say, 'This far, no further.' Sometimes Mary thought fancifully that Joanna was like one of those gorgeous French confections that Richard brought her from Paris—melting and tempting outside but with a small hard nutty centre on which you could damage your teeth if you didn't know it was there.

'Oh, yes, she's agreed.' Richard spooned up the last crumbs of apple tart. 'She's going down tomorrow to meet our prospective purchaser. She's a sensible girl and she puts the interests of the firm before any personal qualms she may have. The villa is likely to prove a bit difficult to dispose of. It's a most desirable property, you know, but it has certain drawbacks. For one thing, you can't get a car up to it and you have quite a climb to reach the place. However, Joanna should manage to sell it if anyone can—as she knows the district so well.'

He pushed back his chair and stood up. 'That, my love, was an excellent meal, as always.' He looked down at his front dubiously and added, 'But I'm not sure I shouldn't start once again being careful with the cream.'

Mary laughed and linked her arm in his as they walked through to the living-room where the coffee-machine was awaiting them on a low table by the fire and the crimson velvet curtains were drawn already, for the May evening was chilly. 'OK, baked beans and cottage cheese for the next few days,' she laughed. They settled down side by side on the sofa and she poured out coffee. 'What *did* happen to Joanna's marriage two years ago—do you know the inside story?'

'Nope, not really.' Richard rested his balding head comfortably against the velvet back of the sofa. 'Only the bare facts. Hubby was one of those macho whizz-kid business geniuses who make their first million at twenty-five. Name of Hal Randall. He bought La Favorita as a holiday home—through our agency. A year or so later it was back on the market—apparently hubby's business had gone bust and everything went with it—the flat in town, the weekend cottage, the flashy car, the Villa Favorita—the lot.'

Mary sighed and her pleasant face was sad. 'What bad luck—I'm glad none of our girls married a millionaire. The higher you climb the further you fall.'

'Exactly.' Richard extracted a slim cigar from a silver case.

'And did Joanna come to you to ask for a job?' Mary's brow wrinkled. 'I can't remember the circumstances.'

'Not exactly,' Richard mused. 'As I recall, she came to the office about the sale of the villa. That was the time that Clarice Smith left to have her baby, and I was looking round for another present-able receptionist. Joanna got talking—I think she needed to unburden herself to someone—and she said that she would have to find work of some kind—I remember being impressed by her. She was obviously going through a bad time but she had a sort of gallantry about her that I liked—and anyway it ended by my offering her the job and her jumping at it. You know the rest.'

'The rest being,' Mary drank her coffee thoughtfully, 'that she's turned out one of the best salesmen—sorry, sales*persons*—you've ever had.'

Richard nodded. 'She certainly has, she's got that essential quality of stickability. To say nothing about being the *second* most beautiful and attractive woman it has been my good fortune to know.' He patted his wife's hand and blew out a plume of smoke towards the ceiling. 'That's why it has always seemed a little strange to me that she walked out on that husband of hers, just when it would appear that he needed her most. Ah well, she's not likely to tell us. Is there another cup of coffee, dear?'

*   *   *

Giles met Joanna off the plane in Nice the following day, looking bronzed and handsome in white trousers and a navy blazer, his fair, sleekly waved hair arranged stylishly. 'This is an unexpected bonus.' He kissed her and took charge of her luggage. 'Good old Richard—he's going to lend you to me when you're through with this sale at Menton, I hear. We'll hit some of the high spots, Joanna. Nice is a great place to enjoy oneself.'

'I thought you were supposed to be slaving away installing computer hardware for the new proprietors.'

'Ah no, I'm arranging for the experts to do that for me. I'm merely the link-man.'

'Crafty!' Joanna's spirits lifted a little as she laughed up into Giles Potter's fair, good looking face.

Giles had joined Europroperties six months ago as its senior agent and from the first he had made it plain that he was interested in Joanna. But he was cool-headed and knew exactly where he was going and he wasn't a man to rush things. He had taken Joanna out to lunch at first, and later they had dined together, but always he had said good night at the door of her flat. That suited Joanna. After Hal she flinched away from any show of passion and Giles was not a passionate man. He knew that Joanna was a friend of the Kilburn family and as he had his eye on a partnership he had decided that marriage with Joanna would be a good thing. Added to which she was extremely decorative and had poise and a cool, remote charm which Giles admired very much.

The only difficulty was that she was still married. Lately Giles had taken to making little quizzing remarks about that. Up to now Joanna had turned off the matter lightly, but Giles was working on it. He had taken care to find out, by tactful questioning here and there, that her marriage had broken down more than two years ago and showed no sign of being put together again.

Giles took her arm as he led her through the crowded airport buildings, carrying her travelling bag in his other hand. 'I've hired a car for you, as Richard asked, and booked you a room at the Hotel de Côte d'Azur in Menton. It's a pleasant hotel—not too plushy. But we can exchange news over lunch—we're going back to the Royale and you can see the place for yourself. It's quite stupendous, Joanna, or rather, it will be when everything's finished. At the moment there are no visitors of course, but the kitchen staff is functioning on a skeleton basis and they've given me a whole suite to myself, would you believe it? The builders are there, of course, but they haven't yet moved in to my floor so I'm living in the lap of luxury. V.I.P. treatment, in fact.'

He grinned deprecatingly but Joanna knew that he was pleased and flattered. Giles loved the sweet smell of success—but what man didn't? Hal certainly had, Joanna thought bitterly. Everything he owned had contributed to his image. Even her.

Hadn't he once promised that he would clothe her in mink and drape her with diamonds?

'Good for you,' Joanna said rather automatically as Giles handed her into a taxi and they drove towards the town.

Giles went on chatting about the hotel but she was hardly listening. As they came within sight of the Mediterranean she was struck afresh by a familiar shock of wonder. The colours! The sea a true, dark sapphire, the rocks brilliant red, the hillside behind olive green making a backdrop for the array of luxury hotels, glowing in candy-colours of pinks and whites. And above it all a canopy of clear, strong blue sky, paling only slightly where it met the horizon.

The first time she had seen the Côte d'Azur was with Hal. They had driven from Nice to Menton to visit Rosa, Hal's stepmother, and Joanna had let out little squeaks of pleasure every time they rounded one of the rocky headlands and a new vista of beauty came into view. 'Oh look—do look, Hal.' She had squeezed his arm in delight until he had warned, 'Hey, steady on, you'll have us in the sea.' But he'd been pleased. He had so loved giving her presents, seeing her pleasure. Stop it, she told herself, pulling her thoughts back. That's all in the dim and distant past and best forgotten. Nostalgia is a self-indulgence that you mustn't allow yourself on this trip.

The Hotel Royale was much as she had expected—a vast, dignified building overlooking the Promenade des Anglais. Its dignity, she saw, was being rapidly overshadowed by a concession to the tourist expectations of today. Workmen were everywhere; walls were being knocked down, carpets ripped up. They passed a fat man in a blue cotton boiler-suit hugging a white plaster statue of a woodland nymph in his arms.

'See what I mean?' Giles smiled as he led the way up the wide staircase whose ornate wrought-iron baluster was evidently destined to survive. 'But I promise you comparative civilisation in my suite.' He squeezed Joanna's arm encouragingly. 'Sorry the lifts aren't working.'

'My suite' was huge and impressive and Giles played host with a flourish, debating with the harassed-looking waiter over the wine list, apologising to Joanna for the *poulpe à la niçoise*, which she thought was excellent. After lunch they sat on the balcony to drink coffee and gaze out over the blue expanse of sea.

Giles lit a cigar, having courteously asked Joanna's permission, and sat back with a sigh of content. 'Now tell me about London. What have you been doing with yourself lately? The only thing I regret about being moved down here is that I don't see very much of you these days, Joanna.'

His voice changed, became deep and meaningful as he added, 'And I want to see more of you, Joanna, much more.'

Oh dear, he was going to get sentimental again and she didn't think she could stand it. It was bad enough having to come here, to all the places where she and Hal had once been so happy, without having another man hinting that he would like to take Hal's place.

She started to tell him about the latest musical she had been to last week in London with Richard and Mary Kilburn, but Giles obviously wasn't listening. He had leaned forward and taken her left hand and was twisting her wedding-ring round.

'Don't you think,' he said softly, 'that it's about time you considered removing this?'

Joanna pulled her hand away. 'Certainly not,' she said lightly. 'A wedding-ring is an insurance policy of sorts, you know. Keeps the wolves at bay.' She laughed, wrinkling her nose at him. There was no point in being crushing to Giles; she had to work with him. And she certainly had no qualms about breaking his heart. She doubted if Giles's emotions ran very deep.

'Ah, but I would suggest putting another ring in its place, you know.'

Joanna laughed again and drained her coffee-cup. 'Thank you kindly, Giles, but I think I'll hang on to the ring I've got for the present.'

She looked down at her slender hand and the broad gold ring that Hal had put on her finger nearly five years ago when she had been just twenty. Sometimes it surprised her that she should be so reluctant to part with it. It was as if, even after all that had happened and after the way Hal had treated her at the end, there was still some tiny spark deep inside her that refused to be quenched completely. The ring had always been a tight fit and now—to have it filed off, brutally desecrated—would seem like killing something that had once had such pulsating life in it.

Giles wasn't going to give up easily. 'Think it over, Joanna. We'd have a good time together. I'm doing well for the firm since Richard sent me down here and it's a super place to live.'

He watched her face for a time and would have been surprised if he could have known what was going on inside her head. Surprised and piqued because it had nothing at all to do with him.

'Ah well,' he said at last. 'I shall go on hoping. At least we've had a pleasant lunch together and you've seen a little of the work that I'm master-minding at the hotel here.' He cleared his throat importantly and got to his feet. 'I wish we could spend more time together today but I'm afraid I've got an important meeting, which is likely to go on and on through dinner, so I think the best thing is for you to make your own way to Menton. I've hired a car for you, it's in the garage. OK? Not too disappointed?' He squeezed her arm gently.

Joanna smiled, shrugging, indicating that business was business. She wasn't in the least disappointed. Ahead of her, tomorrow, loomed an experience that was going to tax the cool, calm exterior she had been cultivating for more than two years, and Giles's company was already striking a jarring note. Giles, she was sure, knew nothing of her connection with La Favorita. To him it was just another house-sale.

In the hotel car park he led her to a small white Renault, put her luggage in the back seat and handed her the keys. 'You're familiar with the route? I've put a map in the glove compartment for you. Probably the quickest way is to get up on to the motorway. You could——'

Joanna shook her head. 'Oh, no, I shall just cruise quietly along the coastal road. I don't care for motorway driving. I know the way quite well.'

That didn't surprise Giles, of course. As one of Richard's sales staff she would no doubt have been in this vicinity before. The fact that she hadn't been here since she had driven these roads with her husband wouldn't occur to him or interest him if it did.

'Well, *au revoir*, then, and good luck with the sale. Keep in touch and join me when you're through with it.

He glanced at his watch. 'I must dash, I'm afraid, my dear. Take care, Joanna.' He kissed her lightly.

She watched him stride away between the rows of parked cars. Before he reached the corner he turned and lifted a hand in salute and she waved back. Then she got into the Renault and slammed the door and promptly forgot all about him.

The sun was pouring down as she eased the little white car through the traffic and out on to the coastal road. So often she had driven this road with Hal, nestling against him happily as he drove their wicked red sports car, the breeze whipping at her fine dark hair until it streamed out behind her. So often she had thought, blissfully, 'I'm the happiest girl in the world.'

She might have known that happiness like that was too good to last. A sudden rush of tears blinded her and the little car swerved dangerously.

Joanna's heart missed a beat as the Renault missed an oncoming car by a few inches and she heard an indignant hooting. Idiot, she scolded herself, what do you think you're doing? Stop drowning in nostalgia, keep your eyes on the road and remember you're driving on the right.

And for the remainder of the drive to Menton she did just that.

Four hours later Joanna sat in the lounge of one of the more modest hotels in Menton drinking her after-dinner coffee and having a small argument with herself.

She wasn't due to meet the prospective buyers of La Favorita—an American couple—until tomorrow and the evening stretched ahead emptily, full of the imminent danger of nostalgia taking over, a danger which she had already encountered. Brooding on the past was just plain silly. You faced it when you had to, and tomorrow she would have to meet it head-on when she visited the villa—but you didn't allow yourself to get emotional about it. So, she argued with herself—the sensible thing was to phone Rosa and, if she were invited, go to her home to see her. The fact that Rosa had a close link with Hal—was, in fact, Hal's stepmother—shouldn't stop her from visiting a very dear friend who had been her mother's friend since schooldays.

Joanna hadn't met Rosa since the break-up with Hal and it seemed a wonderful opportunity to see her again. She had no idea where Hal was and it would be too much of a coincidence if he just happened to be visiting Rosa at the same time— if, indeed, he ever did these days. She supposed that some day she might encounter him again, but she hoped that that day would be as far ahead as possible. But it would be cowardly to avoid Rosa when she was, for the first time for years, so near to her home.

Something was nagging at the back of her mind, something she needed to find out from Rosa, if she had the nerve to ask. She had to know about Hal, she had to find out where he was, what he was doing and—most vital of all—if he had another woman in his life. If she knew that he had it would mean that she must finally cut him out of her life for good and start to plan her future. It might hurt, just a little, but a clean break would be better than this untidy situation. Yes, she would get in touch with Rosa.

Purposefully she stood up and crossed the lounge to the telephone-room, not oblivious to the bold glances coming from the direction of a table where three Italian men were sitting with drinks, their eyes fixed on the way the lavender jersey dress clung to small, pretty breasts and swung round long, slender legs. Joanna was quite accustomed to receiving interested male glances— and often more than glances. Her response was calculated to freeze at ten paces and usually did.

Rosa answered the phone herself. 'Joanna—

what a lovely, lovely surprise! Where are you, darling?'

Only when she heard the warmth in Rosa's voice did Joanna realise how nervous she had been about the response she might receive from Hal's stepmother. 'Guess where, Rosa. I'm in Menton—not ten minutes' walk away from you.'

There was a smothered hoot of glad surprise from the other end of the line. 'My dear girl—how absolutely marvellous. Come along straight away. I'm all alone. Goodness, this is splendid, I can't believe it. Hurry up now, don't waste a second.'

Joanna put down the phone and drew in a deep breath. Well, she had done it, she had taken the plunge. Now she must go ahead and find out whether there was still any possibility of mending her marriage.

Reason told her that she was a fool. Pride told her that Hal had sent her out of his life and she should never forgive or forget. But something deeper than either whispered that they had once had something so good, and that miracles had been known to happen.

As she climbed the steep narrow road to Rosa's home she knew that she was hoping for a miracle.

CHAPTER TWO

ROSA lived in a top-floor studio in a tall ochre-coloured house with peeling paint, wooden shutters and a tiny wrought-iron balcony in Menton's old town. When her diplomat husband—Hal's father—was alive they had lived in Paris and travelled the world, but after his death, five years ago, Rosa had decided at fifty-plus, to start an entirely new life, devoting herself to developing a gift for art which she had never had the opportunity to do before. Menton, the town on the French-Italian frontier, was her chosen place to live, and the old town her chosen district.

She was waiting outside the house as Joanna toiled up the final steps, and as soon as Joanna saw her she knew that her doubts about how Rosa would feel about her had been baseless. Rosa hugged her affectionately. 'Darling Jo, this is such a wonderful surprise. Let me look at you.' She held the girl at arm's length and surveyed her in the yellow street-light. 'More beautiful than ever, but too thin,' she announced finally.

'I'd be even thinner if I had to climb up here very often.' Joanna puffed exaggeratedly to hide the fact that the sight of Rosa brought back so vividly the last time she and Hal had been here together, and made her inside go hollow. She hadn't expected that purely physical reaction. It was just the first touch on a deeply buried nerve, she told herself. Next time she would be more prepared. 'Why do you have to live at the top of a mountain?' she grumbled, laughing.

'Keeps me fit,' Rosa declared as they climbed up the narrow staircase to the top floor. 'Come along in.'

In contrast to the house's shabby exterior the living-room was luxury itself: deep arm-chairs, soft carpets, muted lighting, crystal glasses and decanter set on a silver tray on a low Georgian mahogany sofa-table.

Rosa took Joanna's light coat. 'You're very wise to put a coat on, the evenings can be decidedly chilly here in May. That's why I thought I'd light a fire, it looks more cheerful, don't you think?'

Joanna sank into a chair with a sigh. 'I'd almost forgotten what a lovely place you've got here.'

Rosa tucked back her straying fair hair and took the chair opposite. 'I've never been very sold on the romantic idea that an artist functions best starving in grotty surroundings,' she chuckled. She held up the decanter. 'This is a new wine I've just discovered which is rather good—try some? Or would you like coffee?'

'Wine please, I've only just had coffee after dinner.' Joanna watched her hostess as she poured rosy-pink wine into flutey glasses, at the same time recounting the story of how she had discovered this small vineyard recently where they used some of their grape-crop for putting down wine for their own consumption and how she had persuaded *madame* to sell her a dozen bottles. She was chatting away, Joanna realised, to bridge with tact the awkward gap that both of them were aware of, the years since the last time they met, and the knowledge that on that occasion Hal and Joanna had been here together, when they were holidaying at La Favorita, married two years but still ecstatically in love.

Rosa hadn't changed at all. She was still the same dear, kind Rosa, her rather plain face redeemed by great, soft pansy-brown eyes and a lovely smile. It was Joanna herself who had changed, who had come to terms with the harsh reality that you could love a man and trust him and think you knew him through and through, whereas actually that man had never existed. The man who emerged when confronted by bad luck and failure had turned out to be a very different person.

Rosa took a chair opposite and raised her glass. 'Here's to you, Joanna. Now tell me what you've been doing—it's been ages. What brings you to my beautiful part of the world?'

'Business, not pleasure,' Joanna told her wryly, and then, because she made it a habit, these days, to tackle difficulties head-on, she added, 'Believe it or not, I'm here to sell La Favorita again—or try to. The man who bought it from—from Hal' (she hesitated only momentarily over saying his name) 'has put it on the market again and my firm is having a bit of a job to find a buyer. It's rather off the beaten track, as you know.'

Rosa was looking a little stunned. 'Well——'

she took a long swig of wine 'this *is* odd, isn't it? I mean——' She broke off awkwardly.

Joanna managed a rather twisted smile. 'Yes, it is rather a facer and I don't mind admitting that I would have preferred some other member of our firm to take it on, but there wasn't anyone else available so——' she shrugged '—it had to be me. Our prospective buyers are an American couple and I'm meeting them tomorrow afternoon and taking them up to the villa. I just hope they'll snap it up straight away and then I can get the job wound up as quickly as possible. I don't exactly expect to enjoy going back there.'

Rosa's brown eyes were soft with sympathy. 'Oh, my dear, I'm sure you don't. I think you're very gallant to tackle it.'

Joanna shook her head. 'Not gallant—just realistic. And nearly three years older—and I hope just a bit wiser—than last time I saw you.' With a sudden, unexpected tremor in her stomach she found that she wanted to ask about Hal. Well—best to get it over with. 'Have you heard how Hal is getting along these days? I often wondered. I'd like to think he had managed to—well, you know——'

Rosa was looking steadily at her, clasping her wine-glass between her two hands. 'Oh yes, I see a good bit of him, he's been living in this part of the world since he came back from Hong Kong. He has an apartment in the new town and he often pops up for a meal and a chat, which is nice for me.' She paused. 'He's changed, Jo. You'd hardly know him for the same man.'

Joanna's mouth twisted. 'I don't think I ever *did* know him. What's he doing with himself? Has he started on his way to another million?' That sounded horribly flippant and Rosa glanced keenly at her as she said, 'I think you must know him better than you think. As a matter of fact, he's got a new business going—still electronics, but on a more conservative and safer basis. He seems to be doing very well.'

Joanna's laugh was brittle. 'Good old Hal—never down and out for long.' She changed the subject quickly. 'I'm sure Mother will be thrilled to hear I've been to see you. She's often said she must make the effort to come down here and see you herself but you know Mum—she's up to her eyes in village doings, and helping Daddy out in the practice as well.'

Rosa sighed. 'I'd love to see her, but it's terribly hard to drag myself away from my little paradise here. Paris is as far as I get these days. I'm going up there tomorrow to visit some friends and do some shopping. But tell me all about your job. It must be fascinating, going round all the gorgeous places in Europe selling beautiful houses——'

They talked for a couple of hours without once again touching on delicate ground. Joanna told Rosa about her work and her travels and later they moved into Rosa's studio and Rosa showed her latest pictures and recounted modestly her quite considerable success.

Joanna admired the paintings with their vivid colours and bold forms and strong black lines.

Richard Kilburn was enthusiastic about modern art and from him she had learned to appreciate pictures that some of her friends found bewildering. 'It's lovely to have a visitor that one can talk to,' Rosa said, propping picture after picture on the easel for Joanna's inspection. 'I haven't had a kindred spirit here since Hal——' She stopped and bit her lip, glancing half-apologetically at Joanna, perched on a high stool by the wall.

Joanna slid off the stool and put her arm round Rosa's shoulders. 'Don't mind,' she said steadily. 'I don't, any more. I loved Hal very much and it was a shattering experience when we broke up but I suppose one can forget anything if one really puts one's mind to it, and that's what I've been doing. So don't let's feel we have to avoid mentioning him, as if he's an unexploded bomb.' She smiled wryly. 'That particular bomb exploded well and truly two years ago.' *And blew my world into fragments that have never quite come together again.*

Rosa reached up and squeezed the hand that lay on her shoulder. 'And I've never stopped regretting it, Joanna. I can't tell you how much I've missed you and how truly glad I am that we've been able to meet up again.'

'I'm glad too. I was a bit scared of coming, you know, I didn't quite know how you felt about me. I thought you might have blamed me for leaving him when he was down and out. I know it must have looked that way.'

Rosa slipped her arm through Joanna's as they

went back to the living-room. 'I never thought of it like that. I know how difficult Hal can be when things don't go his way.'

'Yes.' Joanna sighed, reaching for her coat.

Suddenly she had a hollow feeling inside. She was leaving and she hadn't plucked up courage to ask Rosa that vital question.

'Rosa—there's something——' She swallowed a huge lump that was hurting her throat. 'Has Hal—this is a bit difficult—I wondered if there was anyone else. I sometimes think we should have got a divorce, but we never did. Now and again I feel that it's sort of hanging over me. Do you know if he's thinking of marrying again? Because, you see, I've got a lot of life ahead of me and I should be thinking of the future.'

Rosa's soft brown eyes were very thoughtful. 'Yes, my dear, I understand. Hal's never mentioned anything about a divorce to me. But there *is* a girl—he brought her here last week for tea. Denise something—I forget her other name. Very attractive, very young, pretty hair colouring, that peculiarly vibrant shade of red. As to marrying—well, between ourselves she made a point of getting me alone and telling me that they were planning to marry when Hal could get his freedom. That was only her story and it may have been wishful thinking. Hal himself hasn't mentioned it to me but he certainly seemed very interested.' She shrugged. 'It's hard to know, isn't it? You've found another man, Joanna?'

Joanna's hand went to her throat. She had half expected this, but now it had happened she felt mortally wounded by the sudden violent stab of jealousy that ripped through her.

She stared at Rosa for a moment. 'H'm?' She passed her tongue over dry lips. 'Oh yes, I've found another man.' Foolish pride made her say that.

Rosa nodded in an interested way, but didn't ask any questions and Joanna didn't volunteer any information about Giles, and Joanna put on her bright, social voice and said she must be getting back to the hotel to finish some paperwork before tomorrow. She kissed Rosa and thanked her and said Yes, she'd come again. But she wouldn't. The part of her life that contained Rosa and Hal was finished.

Now she knew. Hal had another girl—a beautiful young girl with red hair. Their marriage was finally ending and soon Hal would be asking for a divorce. As she walked slowly back to the hotel, down the steps in the narrow darkened street, Joanna admitted to herself that she had been dimly hoping for some miracle that would wipe out all the pain and misery and somehow put things right between herself and Hal.

Now she had to face the truth that life is composed of facts, not miracles. Hal had gone out of her life, that was the fact she had to come to terms with. And she would. Eventually— somehow—she would.

The following afternoon Joanna was sitting behind a potted palm in the reception lounge of her hotel in Menton, and between its spiky leaves she saw the couple coming through the entrance door before they saw her. The man, in a white alpaca suit, was short and thickset, his red-veined face topped by a huge stetson, which he did not remove on entering the hotel. The woman beside him, presumably his wife, was as plump as a pin-cushion and wore a dress with a large splashy pattern which was at least two sizes too small for her. She would have been very attractive if she had lost a couple of stone. How on earth was she going to get these two up to the villa? Joanna asked herself. The woman, certainly, wouldn't easily manage the climb up the long flight of steps that formed the only access to the villa.

Just for a moment she toyed with the thought that she could explain the difficulty of access and perhaps they would decide that the property wouldn't suit them and there would be no point in going up to inspect it. The prospect of returning to the place where she and Hal had once been happy had been playing havoc with her composure all morning.

She had put in the morning interviewing a removal firm about the shipment out to Canada of the personal belongings of the vendors of the Villa Favorita and promised to contact the firm again when she had time to sort things out. After that she had wandered along the sea-front, trying to think of anything but the afternoon ahead. But it had kept coming back into her mind and every time she thought of it she had had a sick, hollow feeling inside.

Now the moment had arrived and she had to see it through, whatever her personal feelings might be about returning to the place that held so many poignant memories for her. She was an agent, and her job was to sell a property. That was what Richard expected of her and that she was going to do to the best of her ability.

She went forward to meet the couple who had just come in. 'Mr and Mrs Honeybone? I'm Joanna Daley, from Kilburn Europroperties.' She held out her hand with a smile.

'Glad to know you, Miss Daley.' Her hand was shaken enthusiastically by Mr Honeybone and somewhat less so by his wife. 'Mrs Honeybone and I are very sorry we couldn't make it on time.' He took out a large red handkerchief and mopped his brow. 'Our business in Nice took longer than we expected. Now, then, where's this wonderful house that we've heard about? We're all geared up to fall in love with it, aren't we, Evie?'

'I guess so, dear.' Mrs Honeybone smiled a little wanly up at her large husband. 'We've been all morning looking at some houses in Nice,' she explained to Joanna. 'It's much warmer here than I expected. Quite like summer.'

Joanna adopted her sales technique effortlessly as they went out of the hotel. 'I have a car here, if you'd like to——' she began, but Mr Honeybone broke in with, 'We'll take our own car, Miss Daley, if that's OK with you. We brought it over with us, we plan to stay in Europe for some weeks.' He indicated a superb black Rolls-Royce

standing in the hotel forecourt. Only the most
expensive car for Mr Honeybone, evidently.

'Right,' Joanna said, walking towards her hired
Renault. 'I'll go first, shall I? The best way is to
take a road that forks up to the left, and then the
frontier post is a short way on from there.'

This is where it all begins, she thought as she
eased the Renault out on to the road, with the
Rolls following behind. She felt the familiar
places almost coming to meet her as she drove
along. The villa was just over the border in Italy
but she and Hal always used Menton as 'their'
town, for shopping and eating out and especially
for visiting Rosa.

Soon they arrived at the big sign saying,
simply, ITALIE. Crossing the frontier was no
problem; there were few cars about and all she
needed to do was to wave her passport at the
guards as they emerged rather lethargically from
their huts. The Rolls wouldn't have any difficulty
either, she guessed, a Rolls-Royce impressed
wherever it went and usually got VIP treatment,
even here on the French Riviera, where there
were probably more Rolls-Royces than in most
other places.

She knew every twist and turn of the road as it
wound its way in a series of hairpin bends up, up
into the hills. As she drove carefully along she
could see the Rolls below, apparently coming to
meet her. It was quite uncanny. The road up to
the Villa Favorita was terrifyingly steep, she
hoped that the Honeybones wouldn't be put off
by it; she wanted this sale to go through quickly

and smoothly, so that she could get away from this place that seemed already to be throwing out clinging tentacles of memory.

Fortunately they didn't meet any cars coming down the hill and at last they arrived at the piazza and Joanna parked the car near the little old church and nipped out quickly as the Rolls drew up alongside.

Mr Honeybone was looking redder in the face than he had before they started. 'That,' he said, 'was some drive.' He chuckled rather unconvincingly as he helped his wife out of the car. 'Mrs Honeybone was quite sure I was going to have us driving over the edge, weren't you, dear?'

Mrs Honeybone ignored his pleasantry. She stood, breathing quickly, looking about her with a frown. 'Where's the house, then?' she demanded impatiently and Joanna's heart sank. It wouldn't be easy to sell anything to this woman. 'I'm afraid we have to walk the rest,' she said, leading the way. 'As described in our brochure, final access to the villa is by way of a short private path. The views are absolutely breathtaking, as you'll see when we get up higher.'

From the piazza a narrow lane ran straight for a time and then started to rise again. Soon the only way forward was by climbing the steps that had been cut out of the ground. Joanna had never counted the number of steps that led up to the villa but there were a considerable number of them. When she and Hal stayed here they would run up the steps like children, laughing and teasing each other, eager to arrive in their own private little paradise. She went ahead rather quickly and her prospective buyers toiled up behind her. By the time they reached the wrought-iron gate of the villa both of them were breathing heavily.

Joanna paused before opening the gate. 'The view from here is marvellous, don't you think?' She waved an arm downwards to where, far, far below, the Mediterranean spread out, a sparkle of deep blue in the afternoon sunshine. It had never looked more beautiful to her and memory flooded back treacherously. She and Hal had been so wonderfully happy here. Oh God, she thought, it's going to be even worse than I expected.

She pushed open the wrought-iron gate, overhung by branches of mimosa, the fluffy yellow globes filling the warm air with their unmistakable sweet scent. February was supposed to be the month for mimosa and now it was May, but there was always mimosa in flower somewhere in the garden. For a moment Joanna closed her eyes, wondering if she were going to faint as the smell of the mimosa set all her nerves quivering. The mimosa had been in flower the first time she had walked through this gate with Hal's arm around her. Ever since the break-up of her marriage she had avoided the flower-shops in London when the mimosa was in season.

There were more steps leading up to the front door, through the wild garden where great succulent plants reared their spiky leaves and tiny star-like flowers in brilliant blues and pinks and yellows poked up from the crevices between the rocks. Joanna took the key out of her bag and pushed it in the lock. For an awful moment she thought she wasn't going to be able to turn the key and walk inside. Then her professionalism took over. She must think of the present, and the job she was here to do.

The small, white-painted villa sparkled in the sunshine, set like a gem among its lush gardens. It really lived up to the description on the brochure. Joanna thought, trying to hang on to her professional approach. She had never seen it look more lovely and inviting. The front door opened straight into the big, airy living-room. She pushed open the door and stepped inside, holding back the door politely. 'Perhaps you'd like to see over the inside first? Shall I show you the accommodation and then, if you'd care to have a look round on your own?' Automatically she began to go through her sales spiel.

She smiled at Mrs Honeybone. 'The rooms are all on different levels,' she began, 'a little like an open-plan bungalow. Do take care of the steps. You soon get used to it, I——' She stopped. Heavens, she must be careful, she had nearly said, 'I found it quite easy myself.'

She turned into the room and caught her breath. She knew from the office records that the villa was to be sold fully fitted and furnished, but she had taken it for granted that the last owners would have changed some of the furniture, put their own stamp on the place; people usually did. But nothing had altered. The room looked exactly the same as it had done the last time she and Hal had packed up and left to return to London. They had had a wonderful week here; everything had been right with their world then. They had planned to come back for another short holiday the following month. But before that could happen the blow fell that was to wreck their life together.

She walked blindly across the marble-tiled floor and stood in front of the window that opened on to a long balcony, running the whole length of the villa, where trailing plants formed a green roof as they twined around wooden supports. The same white table where she and Hal had lingered over their meals, the same chairs——

Her hands fumbled with the catch of the window. 'It's rather—hot indoors,' she murmured faintly. 'The house has been closed up recently.'

Mr Honeybone released the catch and pulled the window open. 'Sure is hot in here,' he agreed. He looked at Joanna's pale face. 'You feeling OK, Miss Daley? Has the heat got to you?'

'The heat's sure got to *me*.' His wife's voice rose peevishly from behind them. She had sunk into one of the cushioned cane chairs by the window and was fanning her damp pink cheeks with the printed brochure.

'There *is* air-conditioning,' Joanna put in quickly, remembering her role. 'I'll switch it on for you.'

Mrs Honeybone shook her head and pursed her lips in an expression that Joanna recognised immediately. No sale this afternoon, that was for sure. 'Don't trouble yourself, we shan't be staying.' The woman gave her husband a warning look. 'Shall we, Portman?'

'But, Evie dear, shouldn't we look over the rest of the house? It seems quite charming.' Mr Honeybone glanced apologetically towards Joanna.

'All those steps outside aren't charming at all.' Mrs Honeybone turned to Joanna. 'It's no good beating about the bush, Miss Daley, I can see straight away that the house wouldn't suit us, so it would be wasting everyone's time to look any further.' She heaved herself out of the chair. 'We'll be getting back to Nice, Portman, to look at those other villas again. Come along.'

Mr Honeybone shrugged, accepting the inevitability of his wife's decision as he had no doubt done many times before. He looked uncertainly towards Joanna. 'I'm sure sorry, Miss Daley. Look, let me fasten that window again for you.'

Joanna stared at him, focusing his large red-veined face by sheer force of will. 'That's all right, Mr Honeybone, I think I'll stay on here for a time and give the place an airing. There are one or two things to check——' Her voice disappeared in her throat. Go! Just *go* and leave me alone, she screamed silently.

'Well, if you're quite sure, Miss Daley.' The man still hesitated, obviously embarrassed. 'I feel we've put you to a lot of trouble.'

'No, really. No trouble at all, it's my job. I'm just sorry the villa isn't what you want.' I'm not sorry at all, I'd hate to think of that woman living here, criticising everything. She made herself smile at Mr Honeybone, who was really a nice teddy-bear of a man.

'Well—well—goodbye then, Miss Daley, and thank you.' He pumped her hand up and down. At last he managed to get himself out of the room to join his wife. Joanna heard their voices as they made their way down the steps outside; a little squeal from Mrs Honeybone, who was most probably proving her point by stumbling against her stolid husband. The steps outside were rather rough. Hal had always intended to get them re-laid, but he had never got around to it. Some time later there was the sound of the car's engine far below, getting fainter and finally dying away altogether.

Joanna stood by the window. She should go back to the town immediately—it was insane to stay here, asking for heartache. But some urge that was stronger than sanity made her stay. Everything—*everything*—was just as she had last seen it. The couple who had owned the house these last years must have liked it just as it was, or else they hadn't bothered to change things. She looked round the long, beautiful living-room. The same cushions on the sculptured cane chairs that were so comfortable to lie back in and watch the sunset. The same colourful rugs on the tiled floor, the same low coffee-table hewn from local wood that she and Hal had discovered with such glee on one of their trips further up into the villages in the hills. Even the picture that Rosa had painted for them still hung on the wall over the drinks cupboard—a bold, vivid abstract that was Hal's favourite.

She wandered out on to the balcony and stood looking down at the swimming-pool, fitted so cleverly into the only flat piece of ground anywhere around. The turquoise water glittered invitingly. She could go down and swim, she thought crazily. There would be nobody to witness her nakedness. No Hal to join her in the shimmering water, holding her locked against his body until it was too much temptation for both of them and they had wandered back to the bedroom, their warm, wet bodies both enclosed in the same gigantic bath towel, the same drugging anticipation of pleasure flooding their senses. Her hands closed tightly now over the balcony rail. Stop it, she told herself, stop being idiotic. Just go over the villa to check everything and then get back to the town and the hotel and sanity.

She climbed the two steps to the bedroom. For a moment she paused outside the room that she had shared with Hal. It would be agony to go inside, but it might also be healing. It might lay the ghost of the past once and for all. She pushed open the door and went in. Perhaps here, at least, things would have been altered. But she saw at a glance that it was exactly as she had known it, the floor scattered profusely with thick blue rugs, the satin sheen of the fitments, the king-size bed with its duvet cover of palest robin's-egg blue that matched the long drapes over the windows.

She and Hal had been here together when the furniture arrived, and when the men had gone, puffing with the exertion of carrying everything on the long trek from the van and up the steps, but beaming happily as they pocketed Hal's generous tip, Hal had taken her in his arms gently as if she were precious porcelain. He had looked down into her face and the blaze of adoration in his eyes had made her feel oddly shy.

'It's—it's out of this world,' she had stammered. 'Thank you for all this, Hal darling. We'll have such wonderful times here. It's so beautiful.'

His eyes had been dark blue pools, shining with pride as he looked down into her face and drew her towards him. '*You're* so beautiful, and you're mine.' He had looked towards the big bed, its mattress stripped of coverings. 'I want you so much,' he had said huskily. 'How about testing the bed before we begin to unpack?'

Suddenly Joanna had shivered, a long shiver that shook her whole body.

'Cold, sweetheart? Let me warm you up.' He had drawn her closer.

She had shaken her head, biting her lip. 'Just someone walking over my grave, as the saying goes.'

'Don't be so morbid, Jo.' Hal had laughed, pulling off his knitted shirt.

'I'm not. It's just that—that everything *is* so perfect already and I'm so blissfully happy I feel I don't deserve it.'

He had turned her to face the long cheval

mirror. 'Look at yourself.' She looked and saw her reflection there but it was Hal's reflected face above her own that her eyes lingered on. His hands had come round and passed over her sleek black hair, traced her smooth cheeks and the curve of her mouth, passed lower to cover her breasts. 'Never say that again.' His voice had been more serious than she had ever heard it. 'You're the most wonderful girl in all the world and you deserve the best of everything. And I'm here to see you get it.'

So long ago, and yet it all seemed to be happening now. It was strange how certain moments stayed in the memory, so vivid that it was as if you were actually living them. Joanna's eyes filled with tears and her hand went out and smoothed the pale blue duvet cover, remembering the nights of love they had shared here. This house had only seen the good times when they were happy together, and it was the memories of the good times that it was reflecting back to her now. She must remind herself of the bad times that followed, and then there wouldn't be this nostalgic nonsense.

But somehow the bad times refused to come back. She wondered fancifully if the villa itself were rejecting them. She really mustn't linger here any longer. She could come back tomorrow to go through the owners' personal possessions, ready to be packed and shipped to Canada. But for today—she had had enough. She glanced in at the kitchen briefly as she passed. So many memories here too. She closed her eyes and Hal was here again, in jeans and faded blue cotton shirt, open to the waist, disclosing his strong, brown body; his long legs astride the pine stool at the breakfast-bar, his eyes shining as deep blue as the sky outside, his brown hair damp from his shower, curling into his neck as it dried. She could feel the crispness of it as she ran her fingers through it, ruffling it playfully, teasing him. She could hear his laughter and her own joining in. She could feel his arms round her, his lips moving urgently on hers.

She went out quickly and closed the door. She must get away from this place before she went crazy. She'd known it might be bad, coming back, but she had never thought it would be like this—Hal was everywhere she looked.

She went back to the living-room to collect her handbag and the keys, and then to the front door. On her way she tripped over a rug and jerked herself upright. Quickly, quickly, she told herself, panicking as if she were escaping from some mortal danger, like a child rushing downstairs from a dark attic, terrified of unknown horrors that might be following her.

She slammed the front door and locked it and then gulped in a long breath of air. Never again— Richard would have to find someone else to sell this place, she vowed. She turned towards the steps that led down through the garden.

And froze, her eyes blank and staring.

It was imagination, of course it was, a trick of the sunlight that threw shadows through the branches of the mimosa tree down there beside the gate—but for a moment she had thought she saw a man standing there, a tall man in jeans and a pale blue shirt. She forced a laugh through dry lips. This was what came of giving in to nostalgia. It had been just weak sentimentality to linger in this house, reliving the past, seeing old ghosts.

She passed a damp hand over her brow and closed her eyes tightly but when she opened them again the figure was still there. As she looked it began to move, began to climb the steps towards her in a dazzle of sunlight. Her eyes glazed and a scream rose in her throat as she stood rooted, unable to move. She had never been so terrified in her life.

Nearer and nearer the figure came, climbing the steps slowly. Now it was just below her. Her fingers clutched at the handle of the door, her body rigid, staring at this shade from the past that she had summoned up.

'No—no—please——' she mouthed silently. 'Go away. Please go away.'

'Hullo, Jo,' said Hal quietly. 'May I come in?'

CHAPTER THREE

TIME stopped as Joanna stood staring down into Hal's face. She needed every scrap of the self-discipline she had taught herself in the last two years. Her heart was thudding, her hands were clammy, her scalp prickling. When she spoke it was as if her voice came from somewhere outside herself. 'What on earth are you doing here?'

'Looking for you,' he said. There was no expression in his voice. He might have been one of those talking computers, she thought hysterically, and struggled against a desire to burst into wild laughter.

Somehow—she wasn't conscious of unlocking the door—they were inside the villa. Hal walked into the living-room. 'My God,' he said, 'they haven't altered a thing. It's exactly as it used to be.'

Joanna heard herself say in a high, false voice, 'Yes, I was surprised too, when I saw it. Do sit down.' She lowered herself cautiously into a chair, her hands on the arms. Her legs were giving way under her and it would be too humiliating if she collapsed on to the floor.

When he was seated opposite she made herself look at him. Yes, Rosa was right, he had changed. He wasn't the Hal she had known, he was subtly different, although just how she couldn't have said. On the surface he was still the same man—

the same strong, intelligent face, the same crisp brown hair, the same long, hard mouth, the same deep-set intensely deep blue eyes, with their long, curving lashes. The eyes were fixed on her now without any expression in them that she could put a name to. He certainly showed none of the shock that she was feeling, but of course he wouldn't be surprised, would he? He knew she was here and had expected to see her. If he'd needed to prepare himself for what must be an awkward meeting he would have done it beforehand. But perhaps it didn't mean all that much to him.

It was up to him to speak and she waited for him to do it but he seemed in no hurry. When she could bear the silence no longer she said flatly, 'You wanted to see me? Was it about the settlement? I thought everything was fixed up ages ago.'

He blinked quickly as if she had surprised him. Then, 'No, nothing to do with that,' he said. 'The fact is that I was speaking to Rosa on the phone last night and she mentioned that La Favorita was up for sale and that you were here handling it for Richard Kilburn. I flew down from Paris. I——' he hesitated '——I thought I might buy it if the price is right.'

That was what was different about him. The old Hal would never have hesitated. The old Hal would have said, 'I want it, whatever the price.' But if he were here in the capacity of a client then at least she could take cover behind her professional mask.

She cleared her throat, trying in vain to swallow the huge lump that seemed to be lodged there. 'Well, of course, the value has appreciated considerably, but I'm sure you would expect that. So far as I can see—after a quick glance round—everything is in good order, and there seems to have been very little wear and tear on the furniture. I shouldn't think the last owners have used the villa a great deal. They're at present in Canada.' She opened her briefcase and took out the glossy brochure that set out in glowing detail the particulars of the villa, including the price. Richard Kilburn believed in putting an exclusive label on the properties he had for sale. None of your photo-copied house-agents' sheets for Europroperties Limited.

Hal took the booklet from her and glanced casually at it. 'H'm,' he said. He was silent again, then abruptly he lifted his eyes to hers and the blaze of blue dazzled her. She had almost forgotten how potent those eyes of his were; they had always had a hypnotic effect on her. 'What happened earlier on?' he said.

She blinked at him, still under the spell of those vivid blue eyes. 'Earlier on?' she echoed stupidly.

'Some people you were showing over the villa? Some Americans, Rosa said.'

'Oh—those. Yes. They decided not to make an offer for the property. Too difficult of access.'

She saw a flicker of a smile touch the carved lips. 'You *have* got the jargon off pat, haven't you, Jo? Are you still having fun being a successful business woman?'

'Yes, if that's how you want to put it, I am,' she said distantly. *This* was the Hal she must make herself remember—the Hal of those last months, who had finally broken her with his taunts and his cruel sarcasm. The Hal she had almost forgotten in her trip down memory lane. Now she could get the thing into perspective and not drown in romantic nostalgia. Hal hadn't changed after all. 'I enjoy my job very much,' she said with cold remoteness.

He reached out and touched her hand. 'I wasn't sniping, Jo,' he said quietly. 'I'm impressed.'

She drew her hand away, careful not to do it too quickly. She wasn't going to let him guess the effect his touch was having on her. Her mind had rejected him, moved on. But her body hadn't forgotten his touch.

She stood up, hoping her legs wouldn't buckle under her. This interview was turning into a refined torture. 'Would you care to look around?' she suggested.

'Yes, I think I would—if you would be good enough to accompany me, to fill in the details, Mrs Randall.'

'I use my own name for business,' she told him coldly, leading the way to the door. 'Miss Daley.'

'Ah yes, of course. Miss Daley. I seem to recall the name.' That flick of a smile again. Damn you, Hal Randall, Joanna thought, her temper rising. She would have dearly liked to walk out there and then, but loyalty to Richard forbade it. If Hal really wanted to buy the villa she must stick with her job of selling it to him.

As they looked over the villa his attitude baffled her completely. They went from room to room, Hal moving with his lazy stride, leaning against doorways, surveying everything with narrowed eyes, apparently summing up the place as a possible buy, just as if he'd never seen it before, never shared those deliriously happy days here with her. Perhaps he really had forgotten, she thought. Perhaps men could put an old love out of their memories without a backward look.

She hung back, shivering inside, as he opened the door of the room that had been their bedroom, but he walked straight in. 'Nice room,' he mused, glancing round. He strolled over to the balcony, tested the window-catch, went outside and leaned on the rail, looking out and down, across the dark green tops of trees and bushes and the half-hidden reddish tiled roofs of other villas, to the blue panorama of sea far below. 'Good view, too.' He came in and closed the window. His glance flicked casually over the wide bed with its pale blue duvet cover. 'Yes,' he said, 'it may suit me very well.'

They walked back to the living-room. 'Thanks for doing your stuff, Joanna, and for your—how shall I put it?—civilised approach. There's no point in keeping up old feuds in this day and age, is there?' He appeared to consider. 'Yes, I think I may go ahead and make an offer for the villa. But I'd like to do the usual thing and have a second look at it tomorrow before I finally decide. If that's all right with you?'

'Perfectly,' she said calmly. 'Would the morning be convenient for you?'

'The morning would be splendid. Shall we meet here at—say—ten o'clock, if that's not too early for you?' He looked at his watch. 'And now I'm afraid I must rush away. Until tomorrow then. Joanna. *Au revoir*.'

He smiled at her, a pleasant smile that he might have given to any casual acquaintance, and ran down the steps to the gate, closing it behind him without a backward look.

Joanna walked stiffly into the living-room and sank into a chair. She felt winded, as if she had been competing in a marathon race and had stuck it out to the last yard rather than give in.

Remember, she told herself fiercely. Remember everything. She had to build a high wall between them before tomorrow morning. She sat back and closed her eyes, willing herself back in time, trying to discover how things had gone so wrong. Had it been partly her fault, could she somehow have avoided it? Had she failed Hal in those awful months after his business crashed?

She had always loved him, ever since that summer when Rosa had come on a visit to Joanna's home in Dorset, bringing her new, diplomat husband and his son, Hal, just about to start his final year at university. Joanna had been fifteen and Hal five years older and she had fallen besottedly in love with him from the first moment that he had taken her hand and smiled down into her upturned face with his deep-set vividly blue eyes, veiled by their long black lashes. It was a wonderful summer that year, hot and sunny, and she had fallen deeper and deeper in love each magical day of walking and swimming and sunbathing. She was hardly conscious of anyone but Hal. If he wasn't with her the sun stopped shining; when he came into a room or strolled across the beach towards her her whole body started to throb with an urgency that half alarmed, half intoxicated her.

She made plans and excuses for them to be alone together—sometimes the plans worked and sometimes they didn't. But when they did work things hadn't turned out as she had hoped. Hal seemed different when they were alone; more silent, reserved, and when she glanced up at his bronzed, handsome face she had felt a twinge of fear.

Then the last day of the holiday came and she and Hal wandered away from the others on that picnic to Studland Bay and lingered in a hollow in the sandhills and he kissed her with a passion she had dreamed of but never experienced.

Her first kiss! Whatever happened in her life afterwards she would never forget that moment. The feel of the warm sand against her long, bare legs; the waving grasses tickling her arms; the sun beating down from a cloudless sky, the sound and smell of the sea. She lay back and smiled up at Hal, holding out her hand to draw him down beside her. A long thrill ran through her as she felt his strong body against her own. Her lips parted as his mouth came down on hers and her arms went up round his neck, her fingers burying themselves in his crisp hair. She had invited that kiss and she knew it, she'd been hungry for it for days. She would have given him anything he asked for.

But all too soon the kiss was over. Hal detached her clinging arms from around his neck and raised himself on one elbow, cupping her chin with his other hand, and looked down into her huge grey eyes, hazy with an emotion that was new and overwhelming.

'You're a pretty witch, Joanna,' he said. His eyes were amused and yet curiously hard and she felt a piercing stab of disappointment. She had longed for him to go on kissing her, to make some sort of promise. 'You're going to break a lot of hearts, but not mine. Not yet, anyway, I have plans for my future. Perhaps when I have made my first million I'll come back and claim you, and clothe you in mink and drape you with diamonds—who knows?' She had hardly realised it at the time, but that was the first glimpse she had had of Hal's driving ambition. Her mother knew all about it from Rosa. That evening when the guests had left, she spoke about it to Joanna's doctor father. 'That young man is going straight to the top of the ladder. He's certainly very dynamic. Too much so, would you say?'

'H'm.' Dr Daley had the usual medical aversion to snap diagnosis. 'If that's the way he functions, then it's how it has to be. I shouldn't imagine he'd be a very comfortable fellow to live with.'

Had his gaze slid momentarily to Joanna,

sitting by the window, her head in a book,
pretending she wasn't listening but actually
hanging on to every word? Had they guessed that
their child had grown into a woman with that
first kiss? In the months that followed she tried
hard not to give herself away (although later she
had found out that her mother had guessed). But
she had never forgotten Hal. He haunted her
dreams through the rest of her schooldays. Her
headmistress had wanted her to go on to
university but she had turned down the idea. If
she left home, then she wouldn't be there if—*if*
Rosa brought her family to visit again. The
possibility of Hal being at her home when she
was away was quite enough to make her decide.

'I'm not really university material,' she had
insisted to her parents. 'I'd much rather take a
secretarial course and help in the practice. You
can't really see me taking part in demos and
marches, can you, darlings?'

Her parents hadn't tried to influence her either
way, and she thought that secretly they were
quite relieved that she hadn't wanted to leave
home. They would have been surprised, though,
if they had guessed her real reason. She was
surprised herself when she came to think about it.
It was really too ridiculous to build a romantic
fairy-tale around a handsome young man who
had gone away to make his fortune and would one
day come back and claim her as his bride.
Sometimes she laughed at herself when she
thought about it, and then she made a point of
accepting every invitation from the local young

men that came her way—and there were plenty of invitations, for Joanna Daley had grown into a beauty.

Two of the young men showed signs of becoming serious; one was a budding accountant, the other making his way up in his father's building company. Joanna's mother quizzed gently and each time Joanna laughed and said, 'No, darling, never in this world.' And that was that.

By the time she reached her twentieth birthday she had begun to wonder sometimes if she was turning into a modern Miss Haversham, who had wasted her life mourning the loss of a lover who never returned. The thought made her laugh but it sent a little chill up her spine. What if she never met Hal again? Or if he had married someone else? But surely she would have heard about it if he had—her mother and his stepmother corresponded at long intervals and sent cards at Christmas. Once there was a snippet of news of Hal.

'That young stepson of Rosa's is turning out as we thought he might.' Mrs Daley lifted her head from Rosa's letter one day at breakfast. 'It seems he's already started his own company. He's quite brilliant at electronics apparently.'

A year later Rosa came back—alone—and stayed for nearly three months. Hal's father had died of a heart attack and Rosa, who had loved her much-older husband very sincerely, came back to her old friend to mourn her loss and make plans for her future.

Having Rosa staying in the house acted upon Joanna like a charge of electricity. She felt vital, bubbling with energy. When she looked in the glass the eyes that looked back at her gleamed like polished pewter. Her black hair had a new gloss, her delicate skin a new flush. One day—one day soon—Hal would come. Rosa had said he would come to fetch her, and Joanna would see him again. Her bones turned to water every time she thought about it. She didn't know how she was going to wait.

It really *was* like a fairy tale, Joanna had often thought afterwards. Except, of course, that they didn't live happily ever after. But from the first moment they met again something had flamed between them, bursting into life like the spring that had been burgeoning all around them in the Dorset countryside.

That first day, after tea, they had walked along the empty beach together where they had kissed all those years ago. Hal had taken her hands in his and looked down into her starry eyes and said quietly, 'You see, I did come back to claim you, like I promised. I haven't quite reached my first million, and I can't quite run to mink yet, but I've brought you this.'

He reached into his pocket and took out an exquisite diamond ring. 'Did you wait for me, my darling Jo?' he said huskily. 'Oh, I hope you did.'

Their wedding had been the event of the year in the small Dorset village. As she stood beside Hal in the little Saxon church, pale and ethereal in a drift of white lace, with the scent of flowers around her, Joanna had felt herself cocooned in love and happiness.

Everything had got better and better. It had seemed to Joanna that her wedding day was the happiest day of her life but as the months passed each day was more blissful than the one before. As Hal's business success mushroomed their lifestyle became more exciting. The penthouse flat in the Barbican was followed by a weekend cottage in Suffolk. When Hal was working Joanna never needed to be alone unless she wanted to. His friends were her friends, smart young couples of their own age, with plenty of money and out to have fun. Lunches, shopping sprees, matinees, and in the evenings parties, theatres, concerts— life went past like a glittering carnival procession.

And then—finally—La Favorita.

Hal had been so delighted with the villa—like a child with a new toy, Joanna had thought lovingly. That was one of the things that had first attracted her to Hal—his single-minded enthusiasm, his tremendous zest for life. She remembered the evening he had come back to their London flat, his blue eyes shining, to say, 'Rosa phoned me today at the office. She's heard of a villa for sale not far from her that might suit us for a holiday home. It's up in the hills above Menton, just across the French-Italian border. Sounds idyllic. What do you say if we fly down tomorrow, darling?'

Buying the villa had seemed to set the seal on his success. Already the penthouse flat, the weekend cottage, the long, sleek, luxury car. But a holiday home on the Riviera was something else again.

Next day, in the empty living-room—this same room where she now sat reliving the past—he had lifted her in his arms and swung her round in glee. 'We *must* have it—it's just exactly "us". Just look at that view, right down to the Mediterranean. We could keep a small yacht here, darling, how about that?' He could hardly contain his excitement as he planned all that they could do with the villa, how they could furnish it just as they liked, money no object.

'Heaven!' sighed Joanna, snuggling close in his arms as they stood on the balcony breathing in the cool clear air with its tang of pine trees. But in those days everything was heaven so long as she was with Hal. And standing there she had realised, without putting it into words, how much this villa meant to Hal. Not just as a holiday home. It represented far more to him than that. It confirmed him as a high-flier, as an achiever. She had always known that Hal was geared for success, hungry for it. He'd never made any secret of his ambitions and it was all part of him, part of the Hal she loved. Dynamic, magnetic, passionate, full of drive and energy.

She had never guessed, in those wonderful early days, at the darker side of Hal's nature— that had emerged later, with painful, disastrous results.

Three wonderful holidays they had spent here—and always just the two of them. Each one a honeymoon, a new delight in each other. It was bliss, for a change, to have no commitments, no appointments. They could please themselves what they did. If they wanted to stay in bed all day there was nobody to phone because Hal had had the phone cut off. Nobody to ring the front-door bell because only Rosa knew they were here and she would never intrude. They were alone in their private Eden, alone to revel in each other through the sun-drenched days, to make love with new delight in each other's bodies, to lie blissfully in the green shade of the balcony, sipping iced drinks in the evening, watching the glory of the sunset.

Then, abruptly, like a house of cards collapsing, it was all over.

It had happened soon after their last holiday here. At first Hal had tried to keep it from Joanna, but of course she had known that something was wrong and in the end the whole thing had to come out, when the bankruptcy proceedings came along. Everything they owned would have to go.

'How? Why has it happened?' Joanna had asked dazedly and he had looked at her as if she were a stranger. 'Because the bloody market collapsed, that's why. And because my dear loyal partner saw it coming and got out in time, taking his capital with him. I could gladly kill him.' His face was so contorted with bitterness that she hardly recognised him.

He had sat for hours with his head in his hands that night. Joanna tried to comfort him but he didn't seem to listen when she told him she loved him and that they would find a way out. 'We're still together,' she had urged, pressing close to him, her arms round him. 'We still love each other. It can't be all bad.'

If he heard her he didn't respond. He shook off her arms and stumbled out of the room and she heard the front door slam behind him. He didn't come back at all that night and Joanna didn't go to bed. She sat in the beautiful living-room of their penthouse flat in the Barbican, staring at nothing, her eyes dry, a terrible emptiness inside her.

He came back the next morning, haggard and unshaven and offered some sort of an apology. They would get through somehow, he said, he would start again.

'I'll help you, darling,' she urged eagerly. 'I'll do everything I can. I'll get a job and we'll find somewhere to live. And perhaps Daddy——'

'No,' he spat out. 'I won't take a farthing from your bloody family. You can go back to them if you're too uncomfortable with me.'

She had always thought he liked her parents; it was a body-blow to hear him speak like this of them. She had to try very hard not to feel mortally hurt, to go on understanding, making excuses for him, but living with him afterwards was like walking on broken glass. Anything she said might start one of the horrible, wounding quarrels, and sometimes she didn't even make the effort to talk at all and they sat in silence until finally Hal would get up and slam out of the flat.

By this time everything had been sold and they

had rented a small furnished flat—just two rooms, kitchen and shower—and Joanna had found a job with Richard Kilburn. She went home to Dorset once—alone—to try to explain things to her parents. They loved her dearly and would have done anything to help and it was so difficult to have to refuse them. She didn't go back again until the final crash came.

At first Hal tried to find work, without success. His business associates had melted away. 'In the rat race you must expect to find rats,' he had shrugged it off cynically. Even their friends, after a short splurge of sympathy, gradually melted away too.

After a time Hal had stopped looking for work; he had stayed at home all day and begun to drink so much that Joanna's generous salary at Europroperties could hardly stretch enough to buy food when the other expenses were paid. She had to ask him to go easier on the whisky and that was the first time he really turned on her with violence.

'I suppose you get a kick out of being the breadwinner?' he jeered. 'So bloody clever, aren't you? Do you enjoy feeling important, mixing with Richard Kilburn's well-heeled customers? Perhaps they take you out to lunch, do they? *Do they?* Perhaps they have other things in mind than just lunch?'

His face was close to hers, his mouth drawn into a sneer, his fingers digging into her shoulders painfully.

'Let me go, Hal, you're hurting me. Of course

I don't enjoy being the breadwinner, you know I don't.'

He had flung her away so that she collapsed on the floor in a heap. By the time she managed to pull herself up he had gone out.

After that the scenes got more frequent, more painful. She stopped telling him that she understood how he must feel. That did no good at all, merely brought from him a caustic retort that he wasn't looking for sympathy, and how the hell could she know how he felt.

After another month, when things got worse instead of better, she felt drained. She had nothing more to say, nothing to give. Everything she said made things worse between them, and at any moment could lead to one of those awful scenes that she dreaded.

Worst of all, he had stopped wanting to make love to her, that hurt more than anything. It was agony that she could offer him the only comfort she knew and be rejected.

One Thursday when she got back from work to find him slumped in front of the TV she said, 'I'm tired, Hal, I need a break. I'll go down to Dorset tomorrow for a couple of days.' She touched his hand cautiously. 'I do wish you'd come with me, they'd love to see you.'

'Like hell they would,' he sneered. 'Perhaps darling Daddy would offer me a hand-out. Wouldn't that be nice?' Then his face crumpled suddenly. 'Don't go, Jo. Please don't go, I don't want you to.'

But she had reached the end of her tether. 'I

must, Hal, I must have a break or I can't go on. Only for two days.'

The following evening, when she had finished work, she took the tube to Waterloo station. It was the rush hour and lugging her weekend bag through the crowds was murder but she set her teeth and battled on until she reached Waterloo, which was seething with commuters. The Dorset train was standing at the platform and Jo heaved her case on to the luggage rack and sank into one of the few unoccupied seats.

She drew in a long breath. She had done it, she was on her way. At the back of her mind was the anticipation of arriving at home, the thought of the warmth and love awaiting her at the end of the journey, the comfort of the old house in the Dorset village where she had been brought up. If only she could be merely spending an ordinary weekend there, like any happily married girl might spend with her parents. If only she didn't have this feeling of failure, of guilt almost.

She sat waiting for the train to leave, staring out through the window at the trail of people drifting along the platform; they looked tired and dispirited, every single one of them, there wasn't a happy face among them. I'm not alone, Jo thought, everyone's got problems, probably some are much worse than mine.

She heard again Hal's voice as he pleaded, 'Don't go, Jo. Please don't go.' Vividly she saw him back in the flat, heating up the meal she had left for him, sitting down alone at the table with the scratched yellow formica top. *Heavens*, she thought, with a horror quite out of proportion to the event, *I forgot to buy coffee. There isn't a scrap of coffee in the flat.* Suddenly that small omission took on the magnitude of a major disaster.

Somehow, she hardly knew how or why, she was on her feet, hauling her bag down from the luggage rack, pushing her way through the press of passengers moving along the train in the opposite direction looking for seats. 'Excuse me— oh please—oh, I'm sorry,' as she lifted her bag and somehow knocked off the bowler hat of a small man in a navy-blue overcoat. She heard a whistle in the distance and pushed even harder, distraught, breathing quickly, her one need to get off the train. How many feet she stepped on she didn't know, but at last she was on the platform and the train was pulling out of the station. She stood like a statue watching it go, her bag beside her at her feet, a lonely, isolated figure, her gaberdine mac belted in tightly round the waist that had got so much thinner in the last few months, her small face white and tense.

A black porter threw her a cheerful look as he rattled past, driving his heavy trolley. 'Bad luck!' He grinned, jerking his head towards the disappearing train.

No, it wasn't bad luck, it was good luck— good luck that she had come to her senses in the nick of time. Hal had asked her to stay and she had left him. For the first time for months he had turned to her and she had rejected him. How could I, she thought, how could I do that to him?

Picking up her bag she began to run back down the platform.

The flat was so quiet that at first she thought Hal had gone out. The kitchen was just as she had left it, so he hadn't bothered to eat yet. She picked up her bag and opened the bedroom door . . .

'No!'

Joanna spoke the word aloud. Opening her eyes she was back in the beautiful living-room of La Favorita. Outside the sun was setting over the sea and a cool breeze was blowing in through the long window that opened on to the balcony. She pulled herself out of the chair and closed the window with hands that shook weakly and stood with her forehead against the glass, staring out.

But she saw nothing of the beauty. She only saw the scene that met her eyes that evening as she pushed open the bedroom door of the shabby flat in London. Hal by the bed—*their* bed—and the girl from the flat above—her red hair hiding their faces, her arms tangled around Hal's neck. She saw again—as if in a horror film—Hal pushing the girl away as she opened the door. She turned and walked into the bathroom and was violently sick. After a time she sat on the edge of the bath, shivering, and Hal came to her there, white-faced and grim.

What followed was the worst scene of all—the worst because there was no anger, only failure and disillusion.

He hadn't tried to explain or apologise. He said wearily, 'It won't work, will it, Jo? You'd better go.'

'Go? You mean——?'

'I mean exactly that. Go—and don't come back. We're finished—washed up.' He turned away, not looking at her. 'Just get out of my life—and stay out.'

Very slowly and without another word she had picked up the weekend case, still lying ready packed by the door, and walked out. Until this afternoon she had never set eyes on Hal again.

That was enough of remembering. She had armed herself against seeing Hal again tomorrow and that was all that mattered. She closed up the villa hastily and hurried down to the piazza where she had parked the white Renault. As she drove down the long twisting hill to Menton she concentrated on her driving. There was going to be one of those glorious rainbow-coloured sunsets, she glimpsed it at intervals between the trees as she drove downwards. Bitterly she thought that even a sunset was capable of being spoiled by memories.

She reached Menton as the lights came on along the waterfront. There was quite a queue of cars coming towards her as she waited to pull across into the hotel parking space. One of the cars slowed and almost stopped and Jo's heart gave a great lurch as she saw Hal in the driver's seat. He looked devastatingly handsome, his skin bronze against the white of his evening suit. There was a girl beside him in the front seat, a gorgeous girl in a black outfit glittering with silver, a girl whose fiery red hair shone like a signal at danger. She was leaning a little against him, her head on his shoulder, her face lifted towards him, glossy lips parted in a smile as she made some remark to him. He laughed, glancing down into her face and touching her cheek briefly.

Denise something-or-other, Rosa had said, and Joanna hated her with a violence that shocked her.

Impatient hooting behind reminded her that her way was clear and she was holding up traffic. She drove jerkily into the car park of the hotel and sat gripping the wheel with aching fingers.

It only needed this. Hal was preparing to buy back the Villa Favorita and take another woman there.

Outrage spread inside Joanna like a corrosive poison running through her blood, burning away all the memories of those first happy days of her marriage, leaving behind only the black, charred remains.

Now, she thought bitterly, now I'm completely armed against tomorrow.

CHAPTER FOUR

JOANNA left the hotel early next morning to drive to the villa. She had spent a considerable time at her dressing-table trying to repair the ravages of an almost sleepless night. The final result hardly satisfied her but it was the best she could do; if she wore sun-glasses the shadows beneath her eyes might not be such a give-away. She dressed in the cream, textured-silk suit she had worn to travel in. It was plain and expensive and fitted her immaculately. With it she wore sheer black stockings and carried a black leather document-case, which doubled as a handbag. A long mirror in her bedroom told her that she looked cool, calm and competent. The appointment with Hal was going to be strictly business and when it was over she would pack up the owners' personal belongings, as arranged, and leave them to be collected by the shipping firm.

The thought of breakfast appalled her but she drank a glass of fruit juice and nibbled at a roll. She would feel more like eating when this interview was over and she got back to Nice. She left her key at the reception desk and set off.

She drove up the steep, winding hill without incident. There was a dark red Citroën parked in the piazza when she arrived there and she wondered if it were Hal's car and he had got here first. Hal's taste in cars had always been on the sensational side and this car was certainly not that. A middle-of-the-road saloon, smart and well-polished, but with nothing particularly dramatic about it. Joanna decided that it couldn't be Hal's car, and that was a relief because she wanted to be at the villa first, to have time to relax deliberately and do some deep breathing before she had to face him.

But it was not to be. He was standing under the mimosa tree when she reached the gate. She felt out of breath and a bit dizzy and wished now that she had made herself eat more breakfast. Her eyes, under the dark glasses, slid away from the tall form in casual jeans and checked shirt leaning against the gate-post, because she couldn't manage to think of him as a stranger—a prospective client. Her senses tingled at his closeness; it was humiliating when she had tried so hard to feel hate for him, but now that she was here, standing beside him, she had to face the stark fact that he was the man she had once loved, and that her body hadn't forgotten his body, however far apart they had grown in every other way.

She forced a cool smile to her lips. 'Good morning, I'm not late, am I?' Pleasant. Businesslike. So far—good.

'We're both early.' Pause. He watched her face under long, dark lashes, the delicate fern-like leaves of the mimosa throwing dappled shadows across his lean cheeks. 'Hullo, Joanna.'

His tone was faintly questioning and she guessed that he was trying to assess her mood and how she was going to conduct this interview. She would put his mind at rest immediately. 'How are you, Hal?' She made her voice bright, thankful that he couldn't see her eyes behind their dark glasses. 'It's odd that we should meet like this, isn't it, but as you said yesterday, there's no point in keeping up old feuds, so shall we get straight ahead with the business?'

She was walking up the steps to the front door as she spoke and now she took out the key and unlocked the door. 'I expect you'd like to poke around on your own, would you? Most people do.'

Thick eyebrows quirked. 'You and I aren't most people, Joanna. No, I'd like you to come with me.'

She shrugged. 'As you please.'

Once again he strolled extremely slowly round the villa and once again Joanna got the impression that he wasn't really inspecting anything. He was certainly not behaving like any potential buyer that she had ever had dealings with before. He asked no questions, he made no remarks, in fact he didn't speak at all. This was a farce and she began to feel angry, but she followed him round as he had asked, keeping a safe distance away so that they wouldn't touch by accident, and tried to avoid looking at him. It would be too ridiculous if she embarked on her sales talk when both of them were aware that he already knew all that was to be known about the villa.

When it became quite obvious that he was

stretching out the inspection beyond all reasonable limits he said, 'I'd like to have a look outside—at the pool, particularly.'

'Certainly.' If he went on like this she'd be hard put to it not to push him into it.

There were more steps down to the pool. Hal stood beside it on the marble surround and stared into the water, clear as green glass. 'I wonder if it needs draining,' he said at last. 'Do you know when it was last done?'

It was obvious that the pool had been drained and cleaned after the winter and that it was in immaculate condition. Hal was simply making conversation. Perhaps he wasn't as calm and nonchalant about this meeting as he appeared to be. But at least he had made an observation that she could respond to, and that was a relief.

'We could certainly check on that and have it attended to if necessary,' she said crisply. 'The last owners left in a rush, we understand. Business affairs took them off to settle in Canada unexpectedly. They had no time to clear up and attend to details and left everything in our hands.'

He nodded. 'I see.'

There was another heavy silence. Then he said suddenly, 'Joanna, sit down, I want to talk to you.' He grasped her arm and urged her down on to the white-painted seat beside the pool. Her inside squirmed as it recognised and registered the touch of his hands. She drew as far away from him as the width of the seat allowed and began to open her document case, her fingers fumbling with the catch.

'Don't bother with that.' There was a sudden touch of masterful impatience that reminded her of the old Hal. He put his hand over hers and his fingers were warm and dry and the familiar male smell of him was in her nostrils, and she didn't think she could take much more of this.

Her teeth were biting into her top lip. 'What do you want of me, Hal? I was prepared to meet you on business to do with the sale of the villa, but I'm not prepared for anything more—personal.'

She made a movement to rise but his grip tightened over her hand, forcing her down. She had forgotten how strong his hands were; sometimes she had teased him, saying he didn't know his own strength.

'This has got to be personal, and you've got to listen.' He paused and then spoke quickly as if he had rehearsed the words. 'I'm quite serious about buying the villa, but when I heard you were here I had to take the opportunity of seeing you—talking to you. I've got to make you understand what happened between us—before.'

'*No!*' This time she managed to pull away from him and get to her feet. 'It's over—finished. I don't want to listen.'

She started to walk up the steps to the villa and he followed her, close behind. 'You've got to listen, Joanna. I know I behaved badly and you've been on my conscience all this time.'

She stopped, turning to face him. Was it

possible that he really was sorry? She couldn't see any softening in his face—he looked grim.

'Coming between you and your sex life?' she said drily.

His mouth hardened, his eyes narrowed and she felt a tremor of fear. 'That's a pretty cheap jibe, not worthy of you. Let me tell you—let me explain——'

Joanna had a sudden picture of glossy red hair spread against a white jacket, of a dazzling smile in a beautiful, sun-tanned face, and a wave of nausea rose inside her.

She turned away and walked on. 'The time's gone for explanations, Hal.' She braced herself for a last painful effort. 'They say that when a marriage fails there are always faults on both sides. I expect I was at fault too, so you see you can make a new start without having me on your conscience. As a matter of fact it suits me very well too. I've been thinking for some time that we should get a divorce. So perhaps you'll put things in motion with your solicitor, and then we can both have a second chance?'

They were inside the living-room again now. Joanna closed the long windows and locked them and then walked briskly to the front door.

Hal followed her. 'Who is he?' he said.

She blinked. 'Who is who?'

'This "second chance" you were talking about.'

'Does it really matter?'

'Yes, it bloody well does.'

'But surely—surely we don't have to go

through all that old legal business of citing a "third party"? I thought—after two years—if we both agree——'

'Who is he?' Hal said again, his voice dangerously quiet.

'Well, if you must know, his name's Giles Potter. He works for my firm and he's in Nice at the moment. I'm going straight back there now.' That should be specific enough. She might have to warn Giles what had happened. If so, she hoped he wouldn't take it as an encouragement.

They stood on the patio outside the front door. It was nearly over now, Joanna told herself. In another minute or two it would all be finished for good. She felt sick and dizzy and the blood seemed to be draining out of her body. There was something alarming in the way Hal was standing there silently, staring at her with a strange, concentrated gaze.

'I think that's all,' she went on quickly. 'Perhaps you'd contact Richard Kilburn, in London, if you decide to make an offer for the villa. You have the phone number on the brochure. You can look over the place again if you like, just close the door when you leave, will you? I have to go now.' She paused to take in a breath. The mere effort of breathing hurt, drawing in air against the ache in her throat. 'Goodbye then, Hal. It'll be better if we don't meet again.'

'Jo—wait——' He put out a hand but she was already on her way. She was running down the steps from him like a scared animal runs from a terrifying predator, stumbling slightly in her need to get away.

If she had kept her poise to the end, if she had been half-way looking where she was going, it might not have happened. It was the third step from the bottom that proved her undoing. Always they had had to be careful of that step, where the root of the mimosa tree snaked across it, pushing up through a crack in the cement like a distended vein. But at that moment being careful was the last thing Jo was capable of. The toe of her sandal caught in the root, she swayed, her arms clutching at air. Then a yellow blur of mimosa rushed towards her as she pitched forward into the iron gate. After that there was nothing.

She came round, moaning faintly, lying stretched out on a bed. Someone was leaning over her, holding her wrist. There was a deep sigh and then a voice said, 'You're all right, darling, you're all right. Just relax.' Hal's voice. She was safe so long as Hal was with her. She tried to smile but her mouth wasn't working properly. She stared up at him stupidly. 'What—what——' she mouthed.

'Shush, don't try to talk, just rest.'

She lay back against the pillow, trying to focus her eyes but everything in the room was moving. She fixed her gaze on the blue Wedgwood jug that had always stood on the writing-table by the window. It was slowly circling round, stopping and then circling back again in the opposite direction. It was very odd; fascinating really, and it made her want to giggle as if she had had too much to drink.

Hal was beside her again, so that made everything all right. He was holding a glass to her lips. 'Drink this, Jo.' He sat on the side of the bed and lifted her head to sip the cold, clear water.

She drank and spluttered. A few drops were running down her chin and he wiped them off gently with his handkerchief and lowered her head on to the pillow again. She was hurting somewhere, she wasn't quite sure where; it seemed to be her left leg but it might have been the right. Her head felt numb and everything was confused and hazy but there was one infinitely comforting thing and beside that nothing else could be really bad. Hal was here, close behind her, she could feel his breath on her cheek. 'Hal—darling——' she murmured. 'Hold me.'

His arm went round her so gently that she hardly felt its weight, only its comforting warmth. His hand was stroking her cheek, feather-light, stroking, stroking. He was murmuring words that she couldn't hear clearly, but she knew they were the love-words that they had always shared. 'Kiss me, Hal darling,' she whispered and his lips touched hers with infinite tenderness. Joanna drew in a long, tremulous breath and was asleep.

Consciousness came and went and the ache all over her body got worse each time. Her head ached too and she felt hot and uncomfortable. She was vaguely aware that at some point Hal was undressing her very carefully, lifting her body and easing her out of her clothes and slipping a nightdress over her head. Then she felt a cool sponge on her face and forehead and that was lovely. He brought her tablets and helped her to swallow them, washing them down with the clear water that came in bottles and had always been such a part of their holidays together here. Hal was being marvellous, she thought hazily; he had never been so gentle and loving. But then, she'd never been ill like this before, had she? She worried a little about how long they had been here and how much longer they had before they must go back to England, but she couldn't remember. Everything was so muzzy, and her head ached when she tried to think. She wanted to tell Hal how sorry she was about spoiling their lovely holiday, and how wonderful he was being to her, and how she adored him, but she didn't know whether the mumbled words made sense or not.

Later she half-wakened again and it was dark and the only light was from a shaded lamp across the room. She could just make out Hal's tall, shadowy figure, slumped in a chair, his head in his hands. Poor sweet, she thought, why was he sitting up? With an effort she drew in a breath and whispered, 'Hal,' and he was beside her immediately.

'Don't—don't—sit there. Come to bed, darling.' Her voice sounded weak and slurred and very strange. He stood beside the bed and his face was in deep shadow. 'I—I want you with me,' she croaked. 'Please——'

He moved away and she heard the sound of a zip being pulled down, the thud of clothes being shed on to the floor. Then the mattress sagged and there was the warmth of his body close to hers, cradling her against him in the familiar way, infinitely comforting. The pain seemed to ease as his arm went round her waist, touching her with such tenderness that it soothed away the hurt. 'That's better——' she mumbled. Hal was here, close to her, so everything would be all right. She sighed deeply and then she fell into a heavy sleep.

Joanna wakened and lay watching the sunlight creeping between the long pale-blue satin curtains. That was strange, the curtains in the hotel room were pink, with flower-sprays. But these curtains were familiar, she was sure of that. Perhaps she was dreaming. She closed her eyes and opened them again and the curtains were still blue.

Her eyes moved over the room, over the luxurious white built-in fittings, the triple mirror on the dressing-chest with its decoration of little cupids, the thick wedgwood-blue rugs on the marble-tiled floor. The bedroom at La Favorita— of course! Her eyes widened in alarm and her scalp prickled. What had happened? She felt as if she had landed in one of those time-warp films where you find yourself back in another part of your life. It was all so chillingly real, but she must be dreaming. She began to pull herself up in the bed and then let out a yell as pain struck and she hurt all over. At the same instant there was a movement on the other side of the bed. Petrified, she twisted her head round a fraction. There was a man lying beside her, his head turned away from her, bronzed naked shoulders showing above the duvet. Joanna let out a strangled scream and all sorts of terrifying thoughts flashed through her mind in the moment that it took for the man to wake and—turn into Hal.

She sank back against the pillows, whimpering, biting her lips in an effort to make sense of this nightmare.

Hal turned towards her and put a hand on her shoulder and she tried to drag away but every movement was agony. 'Jo—Jo dear?'

He seemed to be asking her something, she didn't know what. She tried to pull herself together. 'What—happened? Why am I here—with you?'

'You don't remember?' His voice was kind, compassionate. 'Then I'd better remind you.' He drew himself up in the bed until he was leaning against the padded back-rest. 'You took a tumble on the steps outside the villa and knocked yourself out. All I could do was get you back in here to bed and wait until you came round.'

Joanna frowned, trying to put detail into the sketchy picture he presented. She remembered now that she had run from him, desperate to get away. Very faintly she had a memory of falling, but after that everything was a blur.

'I can't—can't——' she whispered.

His hand was still warm on her shoulder and it

felt wonderful and somehow—right, and yet she knew that it shouldn't be, that he shouldn't be here, with her at all, that something was very wrong.

'I don't understand—why are you in bed with me? I——'

'Oh, don't worry about that, Jo. Desperate calamities need desperate measures, don't they say? You needed comfort last night and I happened to be here, that's all there was to it.' His blue eyes met hers mockingly. 'You don't think I'd take advantage of a lady who wasn't at all clear what she was doing, do you?'

'You're not saying that I——'

'That you invited me into your bed? Certainly you did, you were really quite pressing about it.' He grinned at her and she felt an odd tug in the region of her stomach. That enigmatic grin of his, the way one eyebrow lifted, touched her with a shock of memory. It was a part of him that she had almost forgotten.

With every minute that passed Joanna's mind was clearing. She remembered now why she had come to the villa—what had happened when she met Hal here—that he had asked her for a divorce and she had agreed promptly. Oh yes, she remembered it all, right up to the moment when she fell on the steps. After that it was just a blur of confused sensations. But she did know that Hal had been kind to her, with the sort of compassionate warmth that she would never have expected of him.

'Well, thank you for your help,' she said

awkwardly. 'I'm sorry to have been such a
nuisance to you, but I'm quite able to manage on
my own now, if you want to get away.'

He lay back on his pillow. 'I don't know that I
do, particularly. I find it very comfortable here.'
He slid a sideways glance in her direction. 'I'd
forgotten how pleasant it is to be in bed with
one's own wife.'

Resentment prickled in Joanna. How dare he
make a joke of everything that had happened?
How could she have believed that he had
changed, become more sensitive?

'I hardly think it's the time for pleasantries,'
she said stiffly. 'And if you want to stay here, I
don't.'

She moved to get out of bed and let out a
muffled yell. The pain was bad enough to make
her fall back in the bed, breathing hard.

Hal sat up. 'We must take a look at the damage.
I'd have got a doctor up here but as you probably
remember we never had a phone put in, and
neither did the present owners, apparently, so
there was no way I could get a medico without
leaving you alone, and that I certainly wasn't
going to do.' While he was speaking he had
slipped out of bed and was pulling on shirt and
underpants.

Joanna tried unsuccessfully not to look at him;
the sight of his naked body gave her a tight
feeling inside. Why did he have to have such a
wildly seductive body, brown and firm, the
muscles rippling in his biceps and thighs as he
moved? She knew every curve of him: there

wasn't an inch of him that her fingers hadn't touched intimately. And suddenly she saw that red-headed Denise's hands caressing him and she choked up. Everything that had happened and was happening served to increase a futile anger that was quickly beginning to turn into a blaze. Anger against Hal, against the situation that had arisen, mostly against her own stupid clumsiness in tripping on that step.

Hal pulled on his jeans and zipped them up, chuckling as he glanced at her averted face on the pillow. 'Not shy, surely? You *have* seen my beautiful body before—remember?'

'Oh, shut up,' Joanna burst out, riled beyond endurance. 'I don't know why you feel you have to make a joke out of this. I can't see anything at all funny in it.'

'Sorry!' He was still grinning. 'I thought it might help—to lighten the atmosphere a little. Now, let's have a look at you.'

He turned back the duvet and perched on the side of the bed. For the first time Joanna noticed that she was wearing a white, pure silk nightie with what looked like hand-made lace round the very low-cut neck. It certainly wasn't one of hers—she'd never seen it before. 'Where——' she began to ask Hal and stopped, wincing, as his hand slipped under her heel and his other hand under the calf of her leg.

He lifted her feet, one by one, flexed her arms, ran his hands gently over her ribs, his eyes on her face as Joanna dug her teeth into her lip, closing her eyes. 'That hurts?'

'Everything hurts,' she muttered. And thought: the feel of your hands on me hurts the most, but not in the same way.

'H'm.' He replaced the duvet carefully. 'We must get a doctor to look at you.'

He stood up. 'I'll make some coffee and then trek down to the town and try to round up a medico. It'll have to be black coffee, I'm afraid. The last incumbents evidently didn't go for tinned milk. There's quite a nice supply of most things in the kitchen though, and the electrics are working. We can manage for a while.' He disappeared towards the kitchen and Joanna lay there helplessly and fumed when she heard him whistling as he clattered about there. What a mess, she thought, what a ghastly mess! And Hal wasn't making it any easier with this display of sweetness and light. He was putting on an act, of course, and she didn't know why—and there was absolutely nothing she could do about it, that was the maddening part.

Still, she told herself, it wasn't for long. If Hal got a doctor here, he would surely be able to arrange for her to be taken down into the town somehow. It might mean an ambulance, she supposed, and men to carry her, because the way she felt now the prospect of walking down to the piazza filled her with horror. She had a picture of being lifted on to a stretcher and her heart sank even further. 'Damn—damn—damn,' she muttered savagely under her breath.

Hal came back with black coffee in two mugs, and a selection of biscuits on a plate. 'Not quite

cordon bleu.' He set the tray on the bedside table.
'I'll do better next time. Here, let me help you.'
He slid an arm carefully under her, lifted her a
little, and propped two pillows behind her head.
The least movement hurt but she tried not to
show it. If she could make light of the injury
when the doctor came it would make the
necessary arrangements much simpler.

'Comfy?' Hal sat on the side of the bed, lifted
the mug and put it into her hand. God, why must
his every touch melt her whole body, in spite of
the pain? 'How do you like my choice of lingerie?'
he went on blandly. 'I had to rifle the dressing
chest to find it. Mrs X had a nice line in undies,
don't you agree?'

Joanna took a sip of coffee and it tasted
horrible. It had probably been in stock for weeks.
Hal tasted his and their eyes met in mutual
disgust. He picked up a biscuit and broke it and it
fell soggily on to the plate.

'The sooner I get down to the town the better,'
he said. 'Just stay put until I come back, Jo.'

She glared at him. 'I can't very well do anything
else, can I? But be quick as you can.' She winced as
the mattress moved when he stood up.

He was watching her face. 'Poor sweet!' He
wasn't smiling now, she could almost believe he
was sorry for her. 'I'll get you some aspirins.
They've left some in the bathroom cupboard—
fortunately they don't go off like coffee and
biscuits.' He disappeared and came back with a
packet and a glass of water. Joanna swallowed
two and grunted, 'Thanks.'

'I'll go then,' he said, but at the door he hesitated. 'Do you need to go to the loo, by the way? I'll carry you in there if you do.'

'No. Just *go*.' She forced the words between tight lips, and he nodded and went out of the room.

Joanna's cheeks were burning. It was idiotic, she supposed, to feel embarrassed when they had shared all the intimacies of married life together, but in a way Hal seemed like a stranger. She lay back and closed her eyes and kept very still while the aspirins began to ease the pain, and tried to make sense of how Hal had changed, coming at last to the conclusion that in a way he had become more—to use an overworked word— more caring. Not that he hadn't cared before, in the early days of their marriage; indeed, he had been wonderful to her, given her everything she could possibly want or need, heaped gifts upon her.

But this was a new kind of caring. More—more human, perhaps. The old Hal had been like a great eagle, soaring up even higher into the sky. Perhaps, she thought fancifully, he had got too near the sun and been scorched when he fell to earth, like Icarus in the old fable. Perhaps he had learnt something, eventually, from that fall. If so, it was a pity he hadn't learned it a bit sooner. As it was, it looked as if the red-head with the moist, inviting lips was going to reap the benefit. She must keep reminding herself of that, Joanna told herself. She mustn't be beguiled into forgetting that Hal planned to bring another woman with him up here, to the Villa Favorita, to *their* place.

Tears filled her eyes and slid down her cheeks. Not because she wanted Hal back. Of course she didn't, she assured herself as she reached for her black case, which he had thought to put on the bedside table, and took a clean handkerchief out to mop her cheeks. She would never, never, *never* risk being hurt again as he had hurt her. It was just that she felt so helpless, and everything was so—so *awful*. For a rare moment, Joanna wallowed in self-pity.

The tablets began to work after a while and she dozed the time away until at last she came fully back to consciousness and saw Hal coming in with a carrier bag in each hand.

He dumped them near the door. 'Iron rations,' he grinned. 'They'll keep us going for a while.' He came over to the bed and stood looking down at her. His face was in shadow but she could see the glint in his blue eyes and felt again that familiar squeezing-up somewhere behind her ribs. 'How's it going, Jo—no worse, I hope? I've managed to contact a medico and he's promised to come up as soon as he can. He seems a nice old boy—an Italian from Ventimiglia—where I did my bit of shopping. I didn't want to waste time going into Menton. I also phoned Rosa but there was no reply and then I remembered that she said she was going to friends in Paris for a couple of days. Well, I can at least make us some decent coffee now. You'd like that?'

'Thank you, yes, I would.' No use being prickly, she might as well accept the fact that she would have to rely on him for everything until she got away. She hoped fervently that the doctor wouldn't be long.

This time the coffee he made was excellent and they both drank in silence, Hal sitting across the room in a cane chair. He had been so chatty before but now he seemed to have nothing to say to her, and when their eyes met he looked away quickly. Her cheeks burned as she contemplated her behaviour last night. Certainly she hadn't known what she was doing; she'd probably been very slightly concussed after her fall. Mary Kilburn had once had a bad fall off a ladder, hitting her head against a cupboard door as she fell and had ended up in hospital with concussion. Joanna remembered her saying that it had been most odd how her memory played tricks on her, wiping out part of her immediate past altogether and skipping backwards in time.

That was what had happened last night. Waking up here, in a room that had been so familiar in the past, seeing the man who had made up all her life then—it was no wonder she had turned to him. It had all been there again, complete, intact—even her own feelings, even the longing for him, the yearning to be close, to feel his hands on her, his arms holding her.

Joanna sipped her coffee and slid a glance towards the man sitting across the room, silent and seeming miles away from her, not just a few yards. Memory hadn't played any cruel tricks on *him*, she reminded herself. He had wanted to see her, to clear things up between them so that he could ask her to agree to a divorce and make a new start with someone else. Everything that had happened yesterday had merely been a tiresome annoyance. Certainly he had been kind and thoughtful but now he must be longing to get her away from here so that he could go on with his own life.

There was a sound from the direction of the front door and Hal jumped up, to return a moment later with a small man with a neatly trimmed grey beard. He was wrinkled and elderly but had a lively look in his black eyes. 'Dr Brazzi,' Hal said to Joanna. 'I'm afraid he doesn't speak any English. Can you manage Italian?' and when Joanna shook her head in dismay he added, 'I'll have to be interpreter then.'

So Hal spoke Italian now; that was something else that was new about him. He stood at the bottom of the bed, arms folded across his broad chest, looking very much the master of the house as the Italian doctor carried out his examination. His touch was light but it hurt abominably as he probed and flexed, uttering staccato observations all the time, of which she didn't understand a word. It seemed that Hal did, for he kept nodding seriously and saying, '*Si. Si.*'

Why couldn't he tell her what the doctor was saying, for goodness sake? When she could get a word in she said hurriedly, 'Please ask him to arrange for me to be moved as soon as possible.'

Hal smiled down at her reassuringly and said

something to the doctor, and there was an exchange of words. Then the doctor took out his stethoscope and went through the usual routine of tapping and listening, running his fingers over her scalp, pausing to examine further when she winced. Finally he took out a pencil-torch and shone it in her eyes, scribbled a prescription and handed it to Hal.

He put his instruments away and clicked the fastening of his bag. Then he took Joanna's hand and raised it to his lips gallantly, murmuring 'Signora.' His black eyes twinkled down at her and he launched into a torrent of words of which she understood nothing, but she smiled and said 'Grazie' which she thought meant Thank You, hoping that he understood her dilemma and would solve it for her. He was still talking volubly as Hal walked with him to the door. They stood outside and their voices came to Jo as she lay, tense with impatience, waiting for Hal to return.

When he did she fired questions at him. 'What did he say? Why didn't you tell me what was going on? I couldn't understand a word.'

Hal sank into the cane chair by the window. 'I'd have thought you'd have got around to mastering Italian in your job, Jo.' He raised his eyebrows, his voice teasing.

'Oh, what does that matter?' She had been attending night classes in French and Spanish. Italian was next on her list, but she wasn't going to explain that to Hal. 'The point is what is he going to arrange to get me away from here?'

'Well—in a word—nothing.'

'Nothing?' Joanna's voice rose to a squeak. 'What do you mean, nothing? Didn't you tell him—explain the circumstances——'

Hal came and sat down on the edge of the bed, taking her hand in his, smiling down at her with maddening complacency. 'Take it easy, Jo. And don't wriggle like that——' as she tried in vain to detach her hand. 'There's a bump on your head which doesn't amount to concussion, although he said it might have made you a bit hazy about things for a time, after the accident. I told him that you'd already passed through the hazy period last night.'

He met her eyes meaningly and Joanna felt her cheeks go hot. 'What else did he say?' she asked impatiently.

'We-el——' Hal raised his eyes to the ceiling. 'He was very firm on the point that you mustn't be moved for forty-eight hours. His first opinion is that there is nothing more than bruising, and that hopefully you should be a lot better by the time he comes again tomorrow. But he can't be quite sure until then and you certainly mustn't attempt to get up until he sees you again.'

'Forty-eight hours?' she wailed. 'But I can't stay here for forty-eight hours. It's someone else's house.'

'Oh, don't worry about that,' Hal said airily. 'As I intend to buy the villa and as the owners are in Canada I think we'll take the risk of being squatters.'

'But what did you say to him—didn't you explain . . .'

'I told him that my wife and I were here on holiday when this accident happened.' He grinned. 'My Italian isn't up to going into all the finer points of the situation.'

Joanna frowned. Hal was behaving very strangely and she had to get this sorted out.

'Now just tell me what's going on,' she said tightly. 'And please leave out the funnies, I'm not in the mood to turn all this into a joke. And let go of my hand and go and sit over there,' she added.

Hal grimaced but did as she asked.

Joanna struggled to keep her voice steady as she said, 'I don't know what your game is, Hal, but it's obvious that you're trying to keep me here in this—this ridiculous situation. You could quite easily have asked the doctor to arrange to have me moved to the town—to hospital—or back to my hotel, or whatever. I'm not suffering from an illness, I only have to rest.'

'Quite.' He clipped the word out. 'And it suits me that you should rest here, where I can look after you.'

'Well, it doesn't suit me,' Joanna burst out, maddened suddenly by his arrogant taking her over, manipulating the situation. 'You're keeping me here against my will as a prisoner, and I won't stay. I'll get away if I have to crawl down to my car on my hands and knees.'

'Very dramatic,' he drawled, 'but not very practical—anyway, I doubt if you could manage to drive down that hill in your present condition. You'd end up going over the edge, which wouldn't be nice for you at all.'

Joanna fumed silently. It was true, of course, she couldn't possibly drive at this moment. She gathered what was left of her strength and shot the word at him, '*Why*, Hal? Why are you behaving like this when things are—are the way they are between us?' She bit her lip hard to stop it quivering. 'You've *got* to tell me. I told you I was engaged to another man and I know from Rosa that you've got another girl. So *why*?'

'Don't you know?' He smiled at her, the slow, intimate sexy smile that had always melted her bones. She could feel it happening now, the familiar turmoil inside, starting low down, moving up and up. Her hands gripped the edge of the duvet. Damn him for having this power over her still.

'Let's say,' he went on, still holding her eyes so that she couldn't move them away, 'let's say that your invitation last night put ideas into my head. Let's say that I'd forgotten how good it is to be in bed with my wife.'

'You wouldn't,' Joanna gasped faintly. 'You wouldn't take advantage—I didn't know what I was doing last night. You couldn't make me—it would be rape.'

'Oh no. Not if the lady were willing. And do you know, I get the feeling,' he added slowly, meaningly, his eyes on her flushed cheeks, 'that she might well be.'

CHAPTER FIVE

JOANNA pulled herself together with an enormous effort. Hal was fooling, of course, amusing himself at her expense, perhaps even enjoying his power over her, helpless as she was—although that didn't really fit in with his character. But what did she know of his character anyway, except that he had proved to be a real Jekyll and Hyde? Two completely different characters in one person: the wonderful, exciting, fabulous man she had first loved, and the bitter, angry, hurtful one he had become later. Now he was choosing to be enigmatic at her expense and that was a new side to him.

Well, it wasn't the time for psycho-analysis and at the moment she had more urgent and practical things on her mind.

She said drily, 'If you wouldn't mind turning your thoughts to mundane matters—I need to go to the bathroom and much as I dislike having to ask you for help . . .'

Hal was on his feet like a shot. 'Of course. I'll carry you.' He turned back the duvet and slipped an arm under her.

Joanna groped at the silk nightie, pulling it down as far as possible. 'I can get there on my own if you'll just help . . .'

'Don't argue.' He put his other arm around

her. 'I'm the nurse, remember? And anyway, you're as light as the proverbial feather.' He lifted her easily and in order to balance she had to put her arms round his neck. His hair was crisp under her fingers and the feel of it brought back all sorts of memories that she would rather have forgotten.

He looked down into her face, frowning slightly. 'You've lost weight, Jo, there's nothing of you. You're all right? Not ill or anything?'

'I'm perfectly well, thank, except for a few bruises and a bump on my head.' Perfectly well so long as I can keep control of my emotions, which isn't going to be easy. Joanna sucked in her breath as Hal carried her across the room. However much she tried to be objective about this it was treacherously exciting to be close to him, the heat from his body passing through the thin silk of the nightdress, his hand firmly tucked under her knees. The churning began again, low inside her. It was so long—so long—and no other man had held her in his arms since Hal. No other man had ever had this immediate effect on her so that an exchange of glances in a crowd, the sound of his voice reaching her through a babble at a party, a casual brushing of hands could set off this tumult of wanting, yearning.

The door of the bathroom led off the bedroom. Hal pushed it open with his foot and carried her inside. 'Here we are then,' he said cheerfully, lowering her with care.

'Want any help—would you like me to wash you?' The blue eyes mocked her.

'No *thank* you.' She hung on to the washbasin and slammed the door in his face.

'Shout when you're ready to come back.' His voice reached her through the closed door, and she thought she heard a chuckle as he walked away.

She sank down on to the bathroom stool, breathing quickly. This was dreadful, this effect that Hal was having on her. She had been so near to losing her control completely out there when she was in his arms, so near to reaching up and putting her lips against his in invitation. Her cheeks burned. What would he have done if she had? Obviously he hadn't been in the least aroused by their closeness as she had, he was making a joke of the whole thing.

It was a tiny bathroom, which was lucky because it meant that she could manage to get from the loo to the washbasin by means of hanging on to the fitments and shuffling along inch by inch. She stripped off the silk nightie and had a sketchy wash, drying herself on the fluffy blue towel that hung on the rail. Even the towels were the ones they had left behind.

Every movement was painful but it was infinitely preferable to having Hal in here to help her. She bit her lip as she remembered how he had undressed her in the night when she was half-unconscious. She slipped into the nightdress again and wondered what she could do about her hair. The mirror told her it was a mess, which wasn't surprising after everything that had happened. She studied her reflection for a moment longer. Her cheeks were flushed, her eyes brilliant, her hair tousled. She looked—she looked as if she had just come from making love. Impatiently she hung on to the washbasin and opened the door.

'Hal!'

He was standing across the bedroom, looking out of the big picture window. He swung round and was at her side in a moment. 'Ready for return transport?'

'I suppose so,' Joanna said reluctantly. 'This is a stupid way to go on, Hal. I've got nothing here, not even a comb.'

He scooped her up into his arms again and lowered her carefully on to the bed. She saw that he had made an effort to tidy it up, smoothing the under-sheet, fluffing up the duvet, straightening the pillows, and the thought struck her that it would never have occurred to the old Hal to do that. The old Hal was a master at reducing a bathroom or bedroom to chaos in the least possible time. Towels in a damp heap on the floor, clothes, shoes, lying where they fell. By the time he left for the office he would be dressed immaculately, but behind him he left a trail of havoc.

'We can certainly provide Madame with a comb.' He took a tortoiseshell comb from the pocket of his jeans. 'Not, perhaps, quite to Madame's standard but the best we can offer. Allow me.'

He sat on the edge of the bed and began to comb her tangled hair, his touch infinitely gentle, avoiding the painful place.

'I can do it myself.' Joanna reached up impatiently to take the comb from him. The rhythmical strokes of his hand were making her feel weak and languid and she needed to keep alert to deal with this situation. She could only guess what Hal's motives were and what he intended to do next, but it was essential that she should keep one jump ahead and be ready for any new move that he made.

'Ah no, let me do it.' He pushed her hand away quite gently. 'I always loved your hair, Jo. Glossy—like a blackbird's wing. Remember those times at the penthouse—how I used to brush your hair for you every night before we went to bed?' His voice was dreamy. 'I loved those summer evenings in London, when we'd sit up there on our balcony and sip our drinks and look down across the river, with the mist and the smell of heat and the day's busy noises quietening.'

'Very poetic.' Joanna managed to take the comb from his hand. 'All that was in another life, of course.' She gave her hair a final couple of tugs and handed the comb back to him. 'Thank you. Now, perhaps, you'll be good enough to tell me what you plan to do. My own wishes don't seem to figure in the matter.'

'Oh, I wouldn't say that.' He returned to the chair and spread out his long legs in front of him, pursing his lips judicially. 'You may have tried to persuade yourself that you'd be more comfortable elsewhere, but if you just think it over you'll see what a rotten idea that is. Where would you go? Hospital? Hotel? Back to dear Giles? I doubt if he'd look after you as well as I propose to do, he's much too busy feathering his nest at the Hotel Royale in Nice.'

'I don't know what you mean,' Joanna said crossly, 'and I wish you wouldn't talk in riddles. What do you know about Giles, anyway?'

'Enough.' Hal's mouth firmed and Joanna knew from experience of that expression of his that he'd said all he intended to say on the subject of Giles. For the moment, anyway. Later she would try to find out how he came to know Giles and what his dark hints amounted to.

He was watching her. 'Aren't you going to ask me what I know about your fiancé?'

'You wouldn't tell me if I asked, would you?'

'No,' Hal said. 'It's a business matter and I don't feel like talking business at the moment.

There was a silence. Then Hal got to his feet. 'I promise to keep you posted as to my intentions.' He grinned. 'At the moment I propose to get you some lunch and then I'll go down to the town and pick up the items on the doctor's prescription. I'll also do a bit of shopping for fresh food. Has Madame any ideas about dinner?'

Joanna's head was beginning to throb, after her excursion to the bathroom and back. Suddenly she was overcome by her own helplessness and tears rushed into her eyes. She shook her head, turning away from him.

'Jo—Jo dear, are you all right? Is it worse?' Hal was beside her, his arm around her, his voice husky. 'I'm sorry, I shouldn't have teased you.

Now, you just lie here and relax and I'll put a bite of lunch on a tray for you.'

He disappeared and she heard him clattering about in the kitchen. He returned after a few minutes with a plate of what looked like spaghetti bolognaise and a bowl of raspberries, accompanied by a jug of cream.

'Not very imaginative, I'm afraid.' He put the tray down on the bedside table. 'All out of tins, but we'll do better when I've been down to do some shopping. I'll be as quick as I can and then we can get going on the doctor's treatment. OK?'

She nodded speechlessly, her head turned away from him. She felt his hand parting her hair and his lips placing a warm kiss in the hollow of her neck. 'Cheer up, duckie,' he whispered. Then he was gone.

When Joanna was sure that he was well away from the villa she let the tears come. It was a long time since she had allowed herself the luxury of tears but now she couldn't stop them. If she had deliberately set out to manufacture a situation that was as painful, physically and emotionally, as the one in which she now found herself she could hardly have done better, she thought, mopping her wet cheeks.

And she had to face the fact that almost the worst part of it was that Hal was being so kind and thoughtful, in spite of the fact that he was keeping her here against her will. He *had* changed. There was still the old strength, the old touch of arrogance, but now there was compassion as well.

And he was even more sexually attractive than ever, damn him. She would have to keep reminding herself about the girl Denise. Perhaps he was meeting Denise even now, in the town. What would he tell her? Would he say, 'Look, darling, a stupid thing's happened. I've met my wife again and she's had a bad fall and I'm having to look after her up at the villa until she can get about again. It's a nuisance, but it will be better for us in the long run if we can keep things pleasant; it'll make the divorce easier. No, of course I don't want her back, my sweet. Anyway, she's engaged herself, so don't worry. It'll be all over in a day or two.'

And what would Denise think of that? It sounded pretty feeble, but perhaps she was so besotted with Hal that she would accept anything he told her. That was how she had been herself at one time. Was *he* besotted with *Denise*? Joanna wondered. And if so why wasn't he putting an end to this ridiculous situation? What did he hope to gain by keeping her here? She had already discounted his remark about wanting her in his bed. That was just Hal's way of avoiding difficult questions that still remained.

There must be some reason for his behaviour— there must be. And she had to find out what it was.

She realised suddenly that she had had nothing to eat since breakfast yesterday morning and, pulling the tray on to her knees, she began to tackle the spaghetti that Hal had warmed up for her. It tasted surprisingly good and when she had finished up everything on the tray she felt less like weeping at her own plight.

But the hours dragged while Hal was away. Yesterday had been quite cool, for early May, but now the weather seemed to have changed and the sun poured in through the wide window and Joanna lay and sweltered and thought longingly of the swimming pool in the garden. They had loved the pool when they used to come here together. She closed her eyes and saw again Hal's bronzed, lean body poised on the spring-board before he dived in, cutting the water cleanly, and powering the length of the small pool to catch her round the waist and pull her under, gasping and laughing. She felt again the way their naked bodies clung and coiled together under the water; the way, afterwards, they lay together on sun-beds in the shade of the leafy, fragrant shrubs that surrounded the pool, and made love slowly, luxuriously, never tiring of the delight they discovered in each other.

Joanna forced open her eyes, blinking in the sunlight that filled every corner of the room. This place was lethal—it acted like a drug, reactivating the past, giving her back the Hal she had adored. She had to make a real effort to bring herself into the present again, but when she heard Hal run up the steps and cross the tiled floor of the big living-room that adjoined the bedroom, she was appalled to find that her heart was beating in great suffocating throbs. This wouldn't do, it wouldn't do at all. She drooped her eyelids and tried to look as if she had been dozing the time away and not anguishing over him.

He strode into the room and dumped parcels on the bottom of the bed. 'Phoo, it's too hot for you in here.' He switched on the fan over the bed. 'Now then—fruit for the poor invalid.' A basket of fruit was divested of its cellophane cover—every fruit that Joanna could think of and some that she didn't recognise piled up into a luscious display of vivid colour. 'And Madame's favourite cologne. Allow me.'

Joanna couldn't resist sighing with pleasure as Hal took a huge bottle of Cacharel Anaïs Anaïs from its packing, removed the stopper and dabbed her forehead liberally with the subtly-scented cooling cologne.

Then he broke a fat black grape from its bunch and popped it into her mouth.

'There!' He stood back, gazing down at her with satisfaction as her teeth sank into the flesh of the grape and the cool sweet juice slid down her throat.

'H'm, that's lovely, you're being very kind,' Joanna said. It would have been churlish not to be grateful, and indeed, she was feeling better by the moment. 'But you really shouldn't have spent so much on me—all this must have cost the earth.' She touched the glittering bottle of perfume.

'I like buying you things, Jo,' he said, and suddenly he was serious. 'It seems a hell of a long time since I've been able to.'

Their eyes met for a moment and Jo could find nothing to say. This was all part of his guilt-shedding process, she reminded herself quickly.

The old music-hall joke of the husband who arrives home late from the office with a bunch of flowers for his suspicious wife. She mustn't—she must not—allow herself to be bewitched by this new, thoughtful, endearing Hal. She must keep on reminding herself how quickly and completely he could change. And keep on remembering Denise, too, of course.

'Everything necessary for the treatment,' Hal said, suddenly cheerful again and beginning to unpack the various small boxes. 'Sorry I've been so long but I thought I'd take the opportunity of calling in at my office while I was in Menton. I have my headquarters there,' he added.

Joanna pulled herself up in bed, wincing slightly. This was an opportunity to get away from personalities. She asked casually, 'And what is your business now?'

He took a labelled bottle out of the parcel and placed it on the bedside table. 'Didn't Rosa tell you? I'm heavily into electronics—the installation side. I've had enough of the manufacturing lark. This way is slower but less risky. Which isn't to say that every new business doesn't have its risks these days. You still have to hope for the big contract that will keep you out of the red. Now let's have a look at those bruises of yours.'

He turned back the duvet at the bottom and tucked a towel under her legs and proceeded to dab lotion on to her hot skin, which she saw was beginning to change from red patches to purplish ones on her legs and thighs. She tried to pretend that it was a real nurse who was performing this service for her, but it was difficult. She had to remind herself that he was obviously not aroused in the slightest by the sight of her body. He was simply obeying doctor's orders. His touch was feather-light and the cool liquid was soothing. 'Oh, that's lovely,' Joanna sighed.

He raised his eyes and met hers and she felt herself flush. That remark of hers, breathed in that tone of sensuous pleasure, had been singularly ill-chosen. Hal chuckled. 'I could do better than that for you, Jo.'

She pretended not to understand and as he soaked a bandage and laid it across her bruised legs she went back to a safer topic. 'Are you working on a big contract at present? Where do you do your installations?'

He replaced the duvet and straightened up. 'Anywhere and everywhere that sees the need for technical up-dating. We've done one or two of the hotels in Menton and a restaurant in Monte Carlo and we're at present negotiating a contract which would be the Big Daddy of them all if we managed to land it. The Hotel Royale in Nice is changing hands—bought by a multimillionaire bloke called Weiss. Have you seen the place, it's a marvellous time-capsule, built in the days when the Promenade des Anglais was first glittering with crowned heads and diadems, so to speak, Weiss is planning to turn it into a show-place for the space age, replanning, re-equipping everything. Which means, of course, the installation of the latest technology. Kitchens—bedrooms—reception areas—restaurants. It's going to be an electronic dream.' He glanced at her as he tidied up the bedside table. 'That's how I met your pal, Giles, by the way. He's grinding his little axe there.'

'He's not exactly my *pal*,' Joanna said stiffly. 'I'm going to marry him.'

He sat down on the bed. 'In love with him, are you?'

'Of course.'

He was watching her closely. 'As a matter of interest, what's he got that I haven't?'

Joanna leaned back against the pillows and closed her eyes. 'Quite a lot,' she said. 'And now, do you mind if we leave the subject? I'm really not prepared to discuss Giles with you.'

'You're probably right.' Hal stood up. 'Giles Potter isn't one of my favourite topics of conversation anyway. Now then, we have to make some plans for our meals for the next day or two.'

Joanna opened her eyes again. 'Day or two? Oh no, Hal, only until tomorrow, when the doctor comes again. After that you *must* arrange for me to be moved if I can't get down under my own steam.'

Hal was on the way to the bathroom, with the bandages and bottles. He stopped and looked round. 'Have you forgotten, Jo?' he said quite mildly. 'The word "must" doesn't figure in my vocabulary.'

Joanna's patience was exhausted. 'You arrogant brute, Hal Randall, I could—I could——' Helpless tears filled her eyes again.

Hal dumped the medical items and returned,

sitting on the edge of the bed again. 'Don't upset yourself, sweetheart, you'll only delay your recovery.' He took one of her limp hands and held it between his own and she didn't even try to pull away.

'I'm not upset,' she said, biting her lip. 'I'm just bewildered as to why you're behaving like this. Bewildered and annoyed. It seems so senseless.'

'You didn't take me seriously then, about wanting you back in my bed?' The blue eyes narrowed. He was leaning towards her and she could see every single hair of his long dark, curving lashes. Treacherously she remembered the way she would close his eyes with the tips of her fingers and plant butterfly kisses on them.

'No, of course I didn't,' she burst out crossly. 'What would happen to that "new start" you said you were so keen on making? And how would Denise feel about you getting together with your wife again?'

His eyes opened wide. 'How do you know about Denise?' he said sharply.

'From Rosa,' she said. 'And I saw you together in a car that first evening. She's very beautiful— and a red-head, of course.' Suddenly, remembering the way the girl had leaned her head against Hal's shoulder, the way he had reached up and touched her cheek, Joanna's control snapped. 'Of course,' she added, 'you always go for red-heads, don't you?'

Hal went very still, the colour draining out of his face as he stared at her and she could see the memory come back to him, the memory of the night they had parted. The night that he had taken a red-head with bold eyes and moist lips into the bed that should have been shared only with his wife. Joanna stared at him, frightened at what she had said and wishing with all her heart that she hadn't said it. It was a cheap, horrid taunt.

He turned away from her and went and stood at the window, his back towards her. The silence between them stretched out endlessly and Joanna sat in the big bed, twisting her hands together and wishing Hal would say something, if only to come back at her with anger. A good quarrel might clear the air. But when he finally turned towards her his face was expressionless. 'There is the answer to your question as to why I'm keeping you here,' he said quietly. 'There are things to be set right between us, some explaining to be done before either of us can move forward again. I tried to talk to you down by the swimming-pool but you wouldn't listen; you walked away from me. Now, by a lucky chance— though you may not see it like that——' he smiled very faintly '—you'll damn well have to listen.'

The playful, enigmatic attitude had gone. Hal was dead serious now, and he meant what he said. She was in no doubt at all that what he wanted was to 'put the record straight' between them. He had treated her badly in the past and some time after that he must have developed a sensitive conscience that nagged at him. Hal had always liked people to think well of him; now he wanted to explain and be forgiven, and then move on to Denise.

She had thought he might have grown up in the two years since they parted, but he hadn't. He was still the small boy, wanting to be forgiven when he had been bad. For a moment the maternal instinct that is supposed to lurk in every woman reared its head and she wanted to take him in her arms and kiss him and tell him that everything was all right.

Then sanity took over again and with it the raw memory of the weeks and months after he had sent her away. The emptiness. The anguish. She shrugged, eyebrows lifted. 'OK then, if you must, go ahead and explain away.'

'In my own good time,' he said shortly. 'And now, we come back to the subject of food. I wonder if Roberto is still running his restaurant up the hill. If he is there shouldn't be any difficulty in getting him to do a take-away for us. I'll go up now and see what's cooking—if anything. You'll be OK?'

'Oh yes, sure, I'll be OK. I'll be fine,' Joanna said bitterly. 'Don't hurry back on my account. Please don't consider me in any way.'

He came to the side of the bed and dropped a quick kiss on the top of her head. 'Nasty temper!' He grinned, and left her.

Joanna lay there, fuming helplessly. There must be a way to get out of this ridiculous situation, there must. But if there were she couldn't think what it was—without a telephone and the nearest villa well out of earshot. No, the Villa Favorita was exactly as Richard's glossy brochure described it—a little gem hidden away in a semi-tropical paradise, far off the beaten track. Richard had really gone to town on that one, she thought crossly.

Thinking of Richard, and business, reminded her of Giles. She wondered if he had tried to contact her at the hotel in Menton last evening, and what they had told him if he had. How long would it be before he began to wonder why she hadn't joined him in Nice, or at least phoned to let him know what was going on? Would he get worried about her if he couldn't contact her? Somehow she couldn't imagine Giles getting in a flap; he was always so suave, so—so smooth. That sounded rather a horrid way to describe him, but he was so much the perfect pattern of a successful salesman that it just had to fit him. She remembered the dinners they had had together; Giles's confident way with wine waiters; his studied attentiveness to her comfort. Oh yes, Giles had perfect manners. She tried to remember what they had talked about over those dinners and, oddly enough, she couldn't remember anything.

Then she came back to the present situation and wondered if Giles would be willing to look after her if she could somehow get to the hotel in Nice. She tried to imagine him being as thoughtful and helpful as Hal was being—and failed. Giles was very, very busy with his important agency work at present and he wouldn't at all welcome having an invalid on his hands.

Oh, bother Hal, she thought crossly. Why did he have suddenly to become caring and compassionate, just when she needed to go on hating and resenting him—and his beautiful red-headed girlfriend? She would concentrate on the negative side of Hal when he returned.

But once again her body seemed to be in total ignorance of what her mind had decided, for when Hal walked into the bedroom, a few minutes later, her mouth stretched itself into a smile of welcome and that familiar quiver gripped her inside at the sight of him, so big and bronzed and—yes—so devastatingly sexy.

'Success, success,' he announced, dropping into a chair and loosening his shirt so that it fell open to the waist, disclosing the thick mat of hair that covered his chest. 'Roberto's still functioning and delighted to see me. He sends his regards, condolences, and all the rest and he's going to send our dinner down when it's ready. He's cooking tagliatelle this evening. Roberto's tagliatelle was one of your favourites, wasn't it?'

'H'm? Oh—oh yes,' murmured Joanna, who had been thrown off her stroke completely by the sight of Hal's bronzed chest and wide shoulders and the way his hair clung damply to his neck, just behind his ears.

'Yes,' she said again, pulling herself together. 'That'll be nice.' And couldn't think of anything else to say.

He regarded her closely, frowning a little. 'Are you OK, Jo? You sound flopped out.'

'Just the heat,' she said. 'I feel a bit sticky, but I'll be better when the sun goes down.'

Hal glanced at his watch. 'There's plenty of time for you to have a shower before our dinner arrives. I switched the water on and it's quite warm. Come along, I'll help you.'

'No, I—I'll be OK.' Joanna shrank back against the pillows.

Hal grinned as he twitched back the sheet. 'You'll feel much better—and more ready for Roberto's excellent food.'

'But I—I can't——' A ridiculous panic was invading Joanna now.

He laughed. 'Can't what? Can't let your husband see you under the shower? It would hardly be a new experience, surely.' Before she could think of any way of stopping him he had lifted her in his arms and carried her into the bathroom. 'This time I won't leave you at the door,' he grinned. 'Now, off with that nightie.'

He was perfectly matter-of-fact about it all and with Hal's arm around her and Hal's laughing voice giving her instructions where to hold on, it became a blissful experience.

He had pulled off his shirt and the water sluiced down over both of them, clinging together in the cool cascade.

'This was always a super shower.' Hal's voice came close to her ear. 'It brings back memories—puts ideas into my head.' The sensation of his wet, naked body touching her own started a slow churning inside Joanna. She tried to wriggle away and nearly fell over in the ffort.

Hal slipped on the wet floor, and straightened himself, gasping, 'What *do* you think you're doing, Jo? Look, my jeans are soaked. I shall have to take them off.' His hand went to the zip.

'Don't you dare,' squealed Joanna. 'Turn this thing off and give me a towel.'

Grinning broadly, he turned off the taps and wrapped her in the big blue towel, dabbing her bruised body dry tenderly, and then slipping the silk nightie over her head. 'There now, that's better, isn't it? We managed very well, although I'm a little damp. A good thing I had the foresight to bring an overnight bag with me when I came back this afternoon.

'Think of everything, don't you?' Joanna said ungraciously.

'I'm thinking all sorts of thoughts at the moment,' he grinned. 'But I must remember that you're a poor invalid.'

'Not for much longer, I'm recovering by the minute.'

'Longing to get back to dear Giles, of course?' He bundled her into his arms and carried her back to the bed. 'Are you suggesting that I should contact him and ask him to come and collect you?'

'No, I'm not. The role of helpless female doesn't appeal, and Giles has enough on his hands at the moment, with the job he's doing, without any more worries. No, when the doctor has been again tomorrow I shall soon be able to get around under my own steam and take up my job again where I left off.'

'And that is?'

'If you're interested, it was arranged that I should join Giles in Nice for a few days and help him out. This hotel sale is a big project, as you evidently know, and he's had a lot of extra administration work to do for the new owner.'

Hal sat down and eyed her blandly. 'Indeed, yes. Giles Potter has a finger in everyone's pie—including mine.'

'What on earth are you talking about?'

'Business matters,' he said. 'You wouldn't want to hear all the nasty little details of what your fiancé gets up to, I'm sure. Let's change the subject.'

'Certainly not,' Joanna said with some heat. 'You've dropped some pretty obvious hints about Giles and you've jolly well got to tell me what you're getting at. I'm just a little tired of your Mystery Man act, Hal.'

He met her eyes in silence for a moment or two. Then he said drily, 'OK, maybe you should be warned what to expect of your future husband. Whenever the Kilburn Agency makes a sale and there's refurbishment of any kind to be done Giles Potter brings in his own boys— cowboys, I should say—and undercuts the perfectly legitimate estimates of the local firms. The lower estimate is usually accepted, the job is done, friend Giles gets his rake-off, and the cowboys conveniently disappear from the scene, leaving the rest of us to pick up the pieces and put all the shoddy work right.'

Joanna stared at him in horror. 'Oh, that's a beastly thing to say. Giles would never behave like that—I'm sure you're wrong.'

He shrugged. 'It's quite well known in these parts. Not dishonest, I suppose, just rather sharp practice. Don't look so horrified, Jo, I'm not trying to brand your boy-friend as a villain. I guess I'm just a bit sore with him at present. He did me out of a job a month or two back, and I've got a pretty good idea that he's going to try it on again with this big contract at the Royale. I'm getting my estimate in soon and it's my guess that friend Giles is already priming his cowboys to undercut me.' He grinned crookedly at her. 'I dare say you're aware of that as you're working with him. We'll end up as business rivals yet, Jo.'

'I don't know anything about it,' Joanna said stiffly, but Richard's words came back to her, even as she spoke. Giles had got himself involved in the installation of a lot of high-tech equipment at the Hotel Royale, Richard had said. All part of the service, of course. Could Giles really be involved with sub-standard work merely to line his own pocket?

Hal got up and came across to stand beside the bed. 'Now look, sweetheart, we've talked enough about business and really it's not your pigeon. It's between Giles Potter and me, if you like, and I'll just have to hope that old Weiss has the sense to pick the best man for the job.'

'It means a lot to you then—getting this contract?' Joanna watched Hal's face. Had he changed at all, or was his drive to get to the top still the most important thing in his life?

He looked away from her, out of the window, and his eyes were deep blue and shining like the strip of sea that she could see from her bed. His mouth was a thin, hard line. 'It means a lot to me, Jo,' he said. 'It means pretty well everything.'

She had her answer then, Hal was still the same old Hal. She was amazed and disturbed that she should feel this sinking disappointment in the region of her stomach. She wasn't quite sure what she had been hoping for in these last hours with Hal, but she knew now that she *had* been hoping. But nothing had changed, she saw that now, the situation was still exactly the same as it had been when he had walked up the path towards her—was it only yesterday morning?

Hal was climbing the ladder to success again with the same single-minded dedication. He knew exactly where he was going and he would no doubt get there. And afterwards—if he failed again it would not be she who would have to suffer—it would be his new love, Denise. Perhaps, thought Joanna very sadly, she would make a better job of it than I did.

CHAPTER SIX

THE sun had set in a brilliant display of apricot and flame, with streaks of green and ragged pools of misty grey, and now the sky was velvet-black. Hal drew a small table up to the bed and spread it with a red-and-white checked cloth. He had even found candles in their crystal holders and lit them and brought in a tiny posy of blue star-like flowers from the garden.

'There,' he said at last with satisfaction, 'how's that for service, Italian style? All we need now is a spot of music. I wonder if the hi-fi is still functioning.' He disappeared into the living-room and a minute or two later the strains of Mozart drifted through into the bedroom.

Joanna lay back in bed and wondered how she was going to bear Hal's play-acting—for that, she was sure, was what it was. They both knew very well that the situation between them was awkward and embarrassing and he was trying to make it easier for them to put a good face on it. She supposed she should be grateful—she didn't think she could stand an emotional scene tonight.

She made an effort to play up to him. 'Very well organised, Mr Randall. You've never considered turning your talents to film directing?'

'It's a thought,' he said. 'If my present business goes bust I'll have a go.'

Joanna was struck dumb. He could joke about his business going bust—it was incredible! Was there anything in their past life together that he was prepared to take seriously?

Just then Roberto's son arrived with their dinner, beaming all over his dark handsome young face and bearing all sorts of flowery messages to Joanna from his father in quite passable English. Also a bottle of rosé wine with the compliments of *il padrone*. He unloaded his tray on to the table, said he would return in the morning for the dishes, and departed.

Hal held up the bottle of wine. 'H'm, *Chiaretto*—definitely acceptable. Very civil of Roberto, I must say. Now, let's get on with it, it looks good, don't you think?'

The tagliatelle with crisp salad did indeed look good and Joanna had to admit that she was starving. 'I can't remember when I last had a proper meal,' she said, 'it must have been—oh yes, I had lunch at the Royale, in Nice, when my plane got in.'

'With Giles?' Hal's voice was mocking.

'Of course with Giles, who else?' She could feel Hal's eyes on her but she wouldn't meet them. She would have liked to mention Denise's name casually, just as casually as he mentioned Giles's, but she found she couldn't.

'You're not really going to marry that fellow, Jo?' Suddenly Hal's tone changed, became almost aggressive.

'Why not?' she said coldly. 'Now let's talk about something else, shall we?'

'Good idea,' Hal said. 'Did Rosa show you her latest paintings?'

Rosa's art activities, and local exhibitions, took them through dinner and as Hal cleared away the plates and lifted the table to one side, filling Joanna's wine-glass again, she began to feel a little less uneasy. 'I'm so glad she's having success,' she said. 'Rosa's a darling.'

'She is that, and more.' Hal lifted his glass. 'To my well-beloved stepmother. I owe her more than I can say.'

He pulled his chair close to the bed, leaned back in it and added, 'D'you know, Jo, Rosa pulled me back from the brink at the worst time of my life.'

Joanna stared at the candle-flame, at the wax that was melting and running down the candles like little fat white snakes. In the flickering light Hal's eyes were dark pools, half hidden by their long lashes. 'I'll tell you a bedtime story,' he said, 'about two beautiful people.' She saw the way his mouth twisted. 'Are you sitting comfortably— then I'll begin.'

He was still play-acting, Joanna thought with sudden anger. Why couldn't he say what he had to say in plain English and get it over with?

He looked up at the ceiling. 'Once upon a time there was a famous diplomat. He had an only child—a son—and he expected the boy to follow in his footsteps. But the son didn't want to be a diplomat, he wanted to be a business tycoon and make a lot of money, and his father was very disappointed in him. They had lots of quarrels.

'He grew up determined to prove to his famous father that *he* could amount to something. His mother had died many years before, leaving some money in trust for him. He took that and set up a business and worked very hard and took lots of risks and they all paid off and he was doing very nicely thank you. He was sad that he could never show his diplomat father what a clever and successful son he had, but his father died before that happened. He put all the money his father left him into the business too, and very soon he was within sight of his first million. Then he met a beautiful princess and they were married, and he loved buying her beautiful clothes, and diamonds, and taking her to exotic places. He was sitting on cloud nineteen—or even ninety.'

Suddenly he stood up and pushed back his chair roughly and began to pace up and down the bedroom. 'Oh hell, Jo, you know the end of the story. I was geared to success and I couldn't take failure. I wanted to give you everything and I could give you nothing. It destroyed me.'

'Not for long, Hal,' Jo said quietly. 'Look at you now.'

He stopped beside the bed and stared down at her, his face grim in the candlelight. 'I treated you bloody badly, Jo, and for two years I've been hating myself for it. That night you came back to the flat—I know what you thought—but it wasn't like that. She came down for some aspirins. I went to get them and she followed me. I didn't want to know. But when you saw us I thought it was an excuse to let you out. I was destroying

you as well as myself. I didn't want that. Guilt is
a beastly thing, it eats into you. I've wanted for a
long time to see you and try to explain and when
Rosa said you were here I couldn't miss the
opportunity. Of course I didn't quite expect
things to turn out as they have done.'

'No,' said Jo, smiling wryly. And then, 'What
do you want of me, Hal?' Oh, please say you want
us to get our marriage together again. Please say
you still love me. She held her breath, waiting.

He spread out his hands. 'I suppose—just to
hear you say you forgive me.'

She lay back against the pillows and looked up
at him, at the long length of him standing beside
the bed, at his shadowed face with the candlelight
flickering on it, at the wide shoulders and strong
muscular chest with springy, dark-brown hair
showing where his shirt fell open. Her eyes
moved downwards over him shamelessly until
they were level with the zip of his jeans, and
slowly, slowly she was melting inside, and the
yearning for his arms, for his kisses—grew and
swelled until she was completely possessed by it
and it was like a living thing inside her, blotting
out everything but her need for him. He was her
husband and she loved him more than life itself
and she wouldn't give him up—not to this Denise
girl, or any other woman in the world.

'I forgive you, Hal, if that's what you want.'
She held up her arms to him. 'Is that *all* you
want?' she breathed softly.

She heard his quick intake of breath and felt
the mattress sag as he bent over her, leaning his

hands one each side of her face. 'You're so lovely,
Jo, so incredibly lovely. Lovelier than ever.' She
could see his eyes now, close to her own as he
gazed down at her, dark blue pools in the
shadowy light. He rested on one hand and raised
the other to stroke the tendrils of dark hair
tenderly back from her face as it lay against the
pillow.

She curled one hand round his neck and drew
his mouth down to hers, parting her lips, moving
her mouth against his seductively.

He drew away a fraction. 'Jo—what are you
doing? We mustn't—we can't——'

'Hal—please—I've been so—so lonely.' She
was almost sobbing now, aching for him to take
her.

'But you're not fit—I'll hurt you if——'

'I don't care. I *don't*. Please, Hal, I can't bear it
any longer.' Her fingers were fumbling with the
buttons of his shirt. With a quick, jerky
movement he wrenched it off, pulled down the
zip of his jeans and then he was beside her on the
bed. 'I'm only human,' he muttered raggedly.
'Tell me if I hurt you.'

Very gently and carefully he lifted her legs and
placed them just as he wanted. Then he raised
her body to slide the silk nightie over her head.
Joanna felt only the merest grumble of pain.
After that there was no pain at all, or if there was
it was swallowed up by the other sensations that
were flooding into her, taking possession of her as
his tongue explored her mouth and moved down
lower and lower until all her nerve-ends were

tingling and the touch of his hands and his lips was arousing an urgent response.

Sometimes, in the past, their lovemaking had been fun, sometimes passionately inflamed, sometimes shamelessly erotic. But never before had Hal aroused her with his slow, gentle tenderness. Her desire mounted to fever pitch. She wanted him closer—closer. She let her hands slide down his body until they closed over his hips, pulling him towards her.

'Now,' she moaned. 'Oh Hal—*now*,' and at last she heard his ragged gasp as he sank deep into her and she cried out with a pleasure so exquisite that it was almost anguish.

They moved together as one body, slipping back effortlessly into the ways they had learned before of giving and receiving the most intense excitement from each other until finally they reached a climax at the same instant and for a long explosive moment stayed suspended there as they cried out in release and then slowly collapsed, panting for breath, legs and arms entwined.

After a time Hal disengaged himself and pulled the duvet gently over Joanna's damp body. 'Mustn't catch cold on top of everything else,' he said. He propped himself on one elbow, looking down at her, a small frown between his eyes. Joanna gazed up at him, waiting for him to say that he loved her, that he wanted to blot out the past and begin again together. For a long moment the silence was heavy in the warm, shadowy room. Then Hal slipped off the bed and pulled on his jeans. He grinned down at her. 'We certainly haven't lost the knack, Jo,' he said wryly, and she recoiled as if he had smacked her face.

He leaned over the bed. 'But I'm a mite bothered about you, I don't think the doctor would have approved of these goings-on. Are you sure I didn't do you any harm, Jo?'

'Quite sure,' she said with agonising brightness. 'I'm feeling much better, as a matter of fact.' The experience they had just shared had reached out to the depths of her being, touched every emotion of love and tenderness. But if he wanted to treat it as a kind of gymnastic exercise, then how could she talk of love? 'Look how much better!' she added gaily.

Draping the silk nightdress round her shoulders she eased herself to the edge of the bed and a moment later was standing on her own two feet for the first time since her accident. Hal made a quick movement towards her but she waved him back. 'See, I can even walk under my own steam. It's wonderful what a spot of sex can do for you,' she added and nobody would ever know what it cost her to smile.

Somehow she reached the bathroom. She turned on the shower and let the spray of cool water beat down on her hot body and mingle with the tears that ran down her cheeks. She was shivering convulsively as she dried herself and the great smudgy grey eyes that stared back at her in the mirror were dark with misery. The bruise on her forehead was turning black and yellow. If she had struck her head in a different place when she fell she might have killed herself. She wished she had. She wished she were dead.

If love were a game, as Hal seemed to believe, then she had played her ace of trumps—but he had thrown down his hand and walked away. She had nothing more to offer; she had given him what he wanted—she had let him off the hook of his guilt about her. She had even polished his ego a bit further by showing him that his sexual appeal was as devastating as ever. She had made a stupid, spineless, pathetic fool of herself.

But no more. The hard centre that Mary Kilburn had recognised in Joanna was spreading until it seemed to be squeezing all the blood out of her. She slipped the white nightdress over her head again. Like a marble statue, she nodded at her reflection in the looking-glass.

Cold as marble. That was good. Marble didn't feel anything, and Joanna didn't intend to feel anything for the rest of the time she was here. Smiling, she walked quite steadily out into the bedroom.

She climbed back into the bed. 'I'm really quite ready to get up and get dressed, but I suppose I'd better obey doctor's orders and stay put until he comes in the morning. Anyway, it's almost time to settle down for the night.' She smothered a yawn. 'I do feel a bit sleepy.'

Hal had pulled back the curtains and was standing in front of the window staring moodily out at the blackness of the night. He turned and came towards the bed. 'Jo——' he began.

Joanna was fiddling with the crumpled lace

round the neck of the nightdress. 'I feel awfully bad about having to raid my client's lingerie drawer. I shall have to do some laundering before I start packing her things up,' she chattered brightly. 'Did I tell you, they have asked my firm to send all their personal belongings on to them in Canada? It's a bit of a responsibility, I shan't be sure how much is personal. What do you think, Hal? Would you like to lend a helping hand?'

'No,' he said. 'I wouldn't.' He stood at the bottom of the bed, frowning, arms folded. 'Jo, I——'

But again she cut in with, 'You know, now I'm nearly better I must get back to the job as soon as possible tomorrow. Giles is depending on me to help with the paper-work in Nice, and I have to report to Richard Kilburn about the possible sale of the villa. Have you decided yet whether you want to buy, Hal?'

'No,' he said.

She nodded understandingly. 'You have to give a lot of thought to a house-purchase—it's always wiser. Perhaps you'll let me know in the next day or two? I'm not quite sure where I'll be staying but Giles has a suite at the Royale and you can always reach me there.'

He spun round on his heel muttering something that she didn't catch. 'I'm going out for a breath of air,' he said shortly.

'Good idea—I wish I could come with you. Our nightly stroll—do you remember—down to the piazza and then up the hill to the little wood.'

She sighed gustily, still smiling. 'How times change!'

Hal seemed to be away for hours, but perhaps it was only a short time. When he finally came in Joanna was lying with her eyes closed. It bothered her that the sound of his footsteps coming towards her should make her heart thump with heavy, suffocating beats, but that was just a reflex action, of course.

She lifted her eyelids sleepily. 'Hullo, you're back. I think I've been dozing, what time is it?' She made her voice slurred.

'Bedtime,' Hal said. 'Would you like a drink before you settle down? Tea? Milk? Ovaltine? Something stronger?'

'No, nothing, thanks. I just want to——' she yawned '—sleep.'

'Take your tablets, then.' He shook two tablets from the bottle and offered them to her, with a glass of water. He was being very practical now, he had dropped the teasing, jokey image he'd been projecting. That was a relief, she wouldn't have to struggle to seem light-hearted herself.

She swallowed the tablets and snuggled down again. Out of the corner of her eye she saw Hal fishing about in a cupboard and pulling out blankets and a pillow. 'W-wha' are you doing?' she murmured.

'Fixing a bed for myself on the floor,' he said.

'Oh dear, that'll be most uncomfortable. But why bother—you can have half the bed with pleasure.' Her chuckle sounded most convincing. 'Don't worry, I won't try to seduce you again,

Hal. You gave me too much wine at dinner, you know wine always had that effect on me.'

He glowered at her from where he was kneeling on the floor, spreading out the blankets. 'You must have noticed I didn't need much encouragement.'

'Well—yes, I did,' she said sweetly. 'It was just one of those things, wasn't it?' she added with an airy wave of her arm, which made the muscles twinge and she had to hold back a gasp of pain.

He punched the pillow on the makeshift bed. 'I'll be OK here,' he said and disappeared into the bathroom. A few minutes later he returned, a towel knotted round his waist, his shirt and jeans over his arm. He tossed them on to a chair.

The candles were still burning on the table beside the bed, the only illumination in the room. He came across and looked down at Joanna. 'Anything you need?' he said and she shook her head sleepily. 'No thanks.'

'Right then, I'll kip down. Good night, Joanna.'

'Good night,' she said.

He blew out the candles and she heard the thud as he flopped down on to the tiled floor, softened only by a blanket. He was going to have a very uncomfortable night, but no doubt he thought it was worth it. He wouldn't want to risk being taken off guard again. Humiliation sent the blood flooding into her cheeks.

Joanna had an utterly wretched night. When you are in black despair you need to be alone at night; to toss and turn and bury your face in the

pillow; to get up and pace round the room; to go
and make tea or put on a coat and walk and walk
in the darkness; all the things that people do in
books and films when they're heartbroken, the
things that seem so corny until you're in the same
situation yourself. Joanna had to lie still, hands
clenched, lips pressed together, and pretend to be
asleep in case Hal should discover that she was
wakeful, and that would be giving herself away.
She had made a fool of herself once, she wasn't
going to repeat the performance.

Somehow the hours passed and she got more
and more tense and her head felt as if a swarm of
bees had taken possession of it. Hal seemed to be
asleep, although she wasn't quite sure. She
remembered that he usually flung himself around
in the bed at intervals when he was sleeping but
now he was lying quiet. He must be regretting
the fact that Italian villas have tiled floors. She
tried to giggle to herself about it, but only ended
up fighting back the tears.

When the light began to creep between the blue
satin curtains she fell, at last, into a deep, exhausted
sleep, and wakened to sunlight and Hal standing
beside the bed with a cup of tea in his hand.

'Sleep well?' he said, watching her face.

'Marvellously. The doctor will sign me off
when he arrives.' She pulled herself up, ignoring
her aching muscles, pushing back her hair and
smiling up at him in a friendly way. 'Thanks for
the tea, Hal. And for everything—you've looked
after me beautifully but I'll soon be off your
hands now. You'll be glad to get back to your

business affairs.'

He tossed off his own cup of tea. 'Oh, they've been ticking over quite well without me. Things are a bit slack at the moment.' She thought he looked faintly anxious. 'We'll be rushed off our feet if we clinch this contract with Weiss, though.'

'When will you know about it?' Joanna said idly. It really didn't concern her but she must at all costs keep the conversation off personal matters.

'Any time now I suppose, as soon as the tenders are in. Tomorrow's the last day and I'll get mine in this afternoon. I expect your friend Potter will be tendering—has he mentioned it to you?'

Joanna shook her head. 'I only arrived a couple of days ago. I don't know anything about the affairs at the Hotel Royale yet, although I expect I will soon, when I get there.' She smiled brightly at him. 'I wish you luck, Hal.'

'Really?' His eyebrows went up.

'Why not?'

She caught a strange expression in his face; he looked almost as if she had hurt him, only that was absurd. He shrugged, turning away. 'Oh, I don't know. I shouldn't have thought you'd have any particularly kind feelings about my business activities.'

There was a rap on the outside door and the sound of footsteps crossing the living-room. The bedroom door was pushed open and the Italian doctor's grey-bearded face appeared round it.

He beamed and nodded and said something to Hal in Italian and then approached the bed. 'Tell him I'm really quite better,' Joanna said quickly and braced herself for the examination.

It didn't take so long today and she was able to submit to it without flinching. Even the bump on her head was hardly painful at all. When he had finished the doctor had a long conversation with Hal and finally turned to Joanna, bowing and smiling, and kissed her hand before he took his departure.

'Lovely manners he has,' Hal remarked to nobody in particular.

'What did he say? Am I discharged?' Joanna asked urgently.

'So keen to end our little return to Eden?' Hal said, his mouth twisting whimsically.

Joanna sat up straight. 'Don't start that again, Hal. You know the score, and I really must get back to work.'

He sighed. 'OK, you win. The doc seems surprised that you've recovered so well. He thinks the danger period has passed, although he suggests that you should go to hospital for a check-up within the next couple of days. Would you like me to arrange that for you?'

'No, thank you,' Joanna said hastily. 'Giles will do that when I get back to Nice—tomorrow probably. I'll be OK to drive by then.'

Hal nodded. 'If that's what you want.' It isn't what I want, she almost screamed at him. I want you to say you love me and won't let me go. But never once in this time together had he mentioned the word 'love'. Never once.

The reply stuck in her throat and she nodded speechlessly, turning her face away from him.

'OK then,' he said briskly. 'I must go down to the office first thing, just for a very short time. You get yourself up and dressed and when I get back I'll help you down to the piazza and drive you to your hotel. See you.' He breezed out of the room.

And that will be the end, Joanna thought bitterly, as she dressed. The episode at the Villa Favorita had turned out even more traumatic than she could have guessed a couple of days ago. She looked round the familiar room and thought fancifully that somehow the villa itself had wanted the two of them to come together again here. 'Stop being idiotic,' she said aloud as she shook out the skirt of her cream-coloured suit and tried, not very successfully, to brush off the marks that had resulted from her fall. She couldn't wear *this* again after today, and she wouldn't want to. It would remind her too poignantly of something that had to be put behind her as quickly as possible. The pain had hardly begun yet but somewhere just ahead she could feel despair waiting for her, like a crouching beast. Despair even blacker than it had been two years ago, because up to now there had been a glimmer of hope, but now the hope was dead.

When she was dressed she went into the kitchen and found the remains of the food that Hal had bought. The kitchen was clean and tidy.

He had even washed up the dishes that Roberto
had sent down from the restaurant last night.
The red-headed Denise was going to have a
model husband! Jealousy ripped through her like
a thin sharp blade and she leant against the
worktop, squeezing her hands against her stomach
until the spasm passed. Then, weak and shaking,
she made herself butter some bread and spread it
thickly with jam to help it down. She must keep
up her strength for the final act of the play when
Hal returned.

She ate, sitting at the breakfast bar in the
sunny kitchen. Then she went back to the
bedroom to tidy up the crumpled bed as best she
could. She was still responsible for packing all
the linen and clothes, she reminded herself.
Somehow she would have to fit that in later—she
couldn't face the prospect now.

She was shaking up the duvet when she heard
steps in the next room, and composed her face
into a careful mask of indifference. 'You've been
quick,' she said, without turning round.

'What the hell's going on here? Joanna?'

She spun round then, and winced as the
damaged muscles rebelled. In the doorway,
immaculate in white trousers and a pink lawn
shirt, his pale eyes vaguely accusing, stood Giles
Potter.

'Hullo, Giles.' Joanna swallowed her surprise.
'You've found me, have you? Did you wonder
where I'd got to?'

He marched across the room to her. 'Of course
I wondered, I've been very worried about you.

Very worried,' he added severely. 'I phoned your hotel last night and again this morning and they couldn't find you, and they seemed to think you hadn't been there for a couple of nights. I had to take time off to come and look for you, although it meant missing a most important meeting. What's been going on, Joanna?' His eyes travelled to the creased pillows and sheet and the duvet which she was still holding in her hands.

She tossed it down on the bed. 'An accident is what's been going on, Giles. I fell down the steps here, the day before yesterday. Fortunately I didn't break anything but I was partly concussed for a time and very badly bruised and quite unable to move all yesterday. The doctor who came was quite insistent that I stay in bed, just in case there was any further damage. But I've seen him again this morning and he's passed me as fit. So I shall resume work almost straight away,' she added, placing Giles firmly in the category of business colleague.

He stood very straight in the middle of the room, arms at his side. 'Well, Joanna, I'm sorry about the accident of course, but I still can't understand why you didn't let me know. And also why you found it necessary to stay here.'

'I couldn't let you know—there's no phone connected,' Joanna explained patiently.

Giles's forehead creased in a pattern of wrinkles. 'I'm quite at a loss. Do you mean to tell me that you've been lying here alone—injured—for two days?'

Joanna sat on the bed, hugging the duvet,

feeling weak. Giving Giles a reasonable explanation seemed to present any number of difficulties.

'Well, I haven't exactly been alone. You see——'

Giles looked shocked as his pale eyes fixed themselves on the crumpled bed-clothes. 'Joanna! What are you saying—have you had someone here with you? Some man?'

'Not *some* man—one particular man,' said Hal, walking into the room. Joanna's inside went hollow as she realised that he must have been listening to at least part of the conversation.

Giles spun round, his mouth falling open. 'Randall! What the bloody hell is all this about?' His fair cheeks had turned an unbecoming pink colour. 'I must ask for an explanation. This villa belongs to a client and should certainly not be occupied.'

Hal stood very still and he looked dangerous confronting Giles, who was at least two inches shorter and almost puny in comparison with Hal's magnificent physique. The antagonism between the two men seemed to crackle in the air as they glared at each other.

'I have been doing my best to look after an injured lady, under difficult conditions,' Hal said, biting the words out between his teeth.

Giles turned to Joanna. 'I don't know what you were thinking about, Joanna, to agree to camp out here. Most irregular. Richard won't be at all pleased about this,' he added pompously. 'And as for you, Randall——' he turned and faced Hal '—you must be aware that you're breaking the law.

You should have informed the hospital and had Miss Daley taken down there. I must ask you to leave immediately. I will take responsibility for Miss Daley from now on.'

'Oh no,' Hal drawled, 'I think I'll finish the job I've begun. And the responsibility for *Mrs Randall* is mine, you know.'

Giles goggled and seemed to have lost his voice. After a pause he muttered, 'You mean— Joanna, is this true? Is Randall your husband?'

'Yes,' said Joanna shortly. 'And I'm very tired of this scene. Please go, Giles. If it's of any interest to you I'll be phoning Richard myself later today, when I get down to my hotel.'

Giles looked from one to the other as Joanna sat on the bed and Hal stood beside the window with his back to both of them, and Joanna could almost see Giles trying to weigh up the situation and see if it could be turned to his advantage.

'Yes—well—I'm really sorry you hurt yourself, Joanna.' His tone was conciliatory now. 'And I'm sorry if I seemed a little brusque with you, my dear, but it was a shock. You know how I feel about you.' He coughed. 'Well—you know where I am when you want me and you'll be joining me at the hotel, as arranged, when you feel up to it?'

Joanna's eyes went to Hal. For a breathless moment she waited for him to say something— anything—that would link them together as a married couple, that would show Giles that he was an outsider. But Hal's back was turned to her as he stood staring out of the window, saying nothing.

She swallowed hard. 'Yes, Giles, I'll be joining you soon, as arranged,' she said woodenly.

'Good!' Giles smiled down at her kindly. 'Don't make me wait too long, Joanna. We shall have a lot to talk about. *Au revoir*, then, my dear.' And ignoring Hal, he turned and walked stiffly out of the room.

Hal turned away from the window. 'Well, now—you're all ready, I see,' he said briskly, as if Giles had never been there. 'We must think about the easiest way to get you down to the piazza. You haven't anything to carry, have you?'

'Only my briefcase.' She stuffed the silk nightdress into it. That would have to be laundered and replaced somehow—as yet she hadn't worked out how she was going to cope with the packing. 'And there's no problem about getting down to the car, I can walk perfectly well.'

He looked at her doubtfully. 'I could carry you if you'd let me.'

'No,' said Joanna sharply. To be held in Hal's arms, pressed against him, her face brushing his cheek, that would be more than she could bear.

There was a knock at the front door and Hal went to open it. She heard him talking to someone and a moment or two later he came back with Roberto's son, the young man who had delivered their dinner last night.

'Giuseppe has very civilly offered his assistance,' Hal said. 'With one of us each side of you we should be able to get you down to the piazza without doing any further damage.'

There was no way that Joanna could object to this and a few minutes later the odd little party set off, Hal on one side of Joanna and Giuseppe on the other. The two men linked their arms round her back, supporting her, and this way they progressed slowly down the steps, along the rough path with its overhanging bushes, down more steps, and finally arrived at the little piazza, where Joanna's white Renault stood waiting.

Hal thanked the young Italian who replied enthusiastically, with much waving of hands and flashing of bold black eyes in Joanna's direction. He then pocketed the note that changed hands and, with a wide grin and a cheerful '*Ciao*', ran lightly back the way they had come.

'Nice lad,' mused Hal, his arm still round Joanna. 'We managed very well. Are you OK?'

'I'm fine.' She began to disengage herself and move towards the white Renault.

'Oh no, you don't.' Hal stopped her. 'No driving for you today, my girl, I mean to get you back to your hotel in one piece. We'll go in my car and I'll arrange for yours to be collected and delivered to you later in the day. Just tell me the name of your hotel.'

Joanna glanced up at Hal's set, determined face and saw that it was no use arguing with him in this mood. She allowed him to lead her to the red Citröen standing next to the Renault and install her carefully in the passenger seat. Hal slid in beside her, placed her black briefcase, which he had been carrying, on her lap, and they drove in silence down the long, winding hill to the frontier post and from there to Joanna's hotel in Menton.

All the time her tension grew as the moment of parting came closer. What would he say when he left her? Could she have been mistaken about his attitude after they had made love last night? As he went to the reception desk to get her room key she found that her hands were damp and she was trembling.

They went up together in the lift and Hal opened the door of her room. He looked round. 'H'm, reasonably comfortable. Now I'd suggest that you have a good rest, Jo, after that exertion.' He sat her down on the bed and pulled off her shoes. Then he lifted her legs on to the bed, pulled the cover lightly over her, and straightened up, smiling down at her. 'You think you'll be able to cope now on your own?'

She couldn't meet his eyes. 'Oh yes, I'll be OK, thanks,' she muttered.

'I'll be getting along then to my day's toil,' he grinned. There was a pause. 'It's been odd the way we've met again, hasn't it? Rewarding, though.' His tone changed. 'You're a lovely, warm, kind girl, Jo, and thank you for your understanding.' He hesitated a moment longer as if he were going to say something else. Then he turned away and she heard the door close with a click behind him.

CHAPTER SEVEN

FOR a time Joanna lay there, limp and exhausted. It *had* been an effort getting from the villa down to the car, although she wouldn't have admitted it to Hal, because the stress hadn't been all physical. Most of it had been the tearing at her emotions at the thought that she was soon going to be parted again from Hal, and this time it would be for ever.

Tears pricked behind her eyelids and she willed them back and pulled herself off the bed. Life must go on and she had a job to do. She would stay in Menton today and rest but by tomorrow she would be quite fit to drive. She would join Giles in Nice and take up her life again where it had left off. Well, not quite where it had left off. The possibility that she might consider marrying Giles had become an impossibility. Being married to any man other than Hal was an impossibility. Very soon she would be a divorcée and that felt strange, but that was what she would remain, so she'd better get used to the idea.

Setting her teeth against the effort she stripped off the cream suit, rolled it up and pushed it into the bottom of her travelling-case. She swilled her hands and face and put on one of the cotton dresses she had brought with her, a crisp lettuce-green linen with wide, white lapels. The green colour made her cheeks look paler than ever and she spent some time putting on a light make-up and arranging her dark hair smoothly to hide the bruise on her forehead. With all this finished, the mirror told her that she looked cool and calm and businesslike. There was no hint that something inside was shrivelling up and dying.

Now—to get back on the job. First she must telephone Richard in London and give him an account of what had been happening. She wasn't looking forward to that; even an edited account was going to sound crazy, and the fact that she had agreed to camp out in a property for which Richard's agency had responsibility could hardly be glossed over.

But no sooner had she heard Richard's greeting at the other end of the line, and plunged into apologies and explanations, than he stopped her. 'Wait a bit, Joanna. I know all this already. Your husband rang me only about half an hour ago and gave me an account of what happened. My dear girl, I'm so sorry about your accident. What a thing to happen—are you sure you haven't done yourself any real damage?'

Richard's familiar voice sounded so concerned and affectionate that Joanna wanted to weep. 'I'm OK, Richard,' she said, and blurted out, 'but I've been so worried about—about the villa and everything.'

'No need, my child, no need at all. Your husband suggested putting the score right by agreeing to a short tenancy, and as the vendors also had that in mind there was no problem.'

'Oh,' said Joanna rather blankly. 'I didn't know—Hal didn't say. I suppose that's all right then.'

'Perfectly. Very all right, I'd say. Your husband mentioned that he will probably be putting in an offer for the purchase of the villa very shortly. It seems that he's rather tied up with a business matter at the moment but when he has an opportunity to go into financial details of the possible purchase he will be in touch with us.'

'Oh,' said Joanna again. She felt a fool because she didn't know any of this—Hal hadn't thought fit to tell her. Of course, Richard wouldn't know what the position was between herself and Hal. Hal wouldn't have told him that they were divorcing—or would he? She didn't know. She didn't know anything. Tears of futile anger gathered behind her eyelids. She was weeping far too much lately, she must stop it.

Richard was saying that she must look after herself and not hurry back to London. Dear Richard, he was being very tactful and skirting round the subject of just where Joanna was going to be, and who she was going to be spending the next few days with.

She must make that clear immediately; she owed it to him as his employee. 'I'll be driving over to Nice tomorrow, as arranged,' she said. 'Giles will be glad of some help with the paper-work, and there's nothing more I can do here in

Menton if the sale of the Villa Favorita is held over for the present.'

'Ah!' A discreet pause at the other end of the line. 'Well, I do wish you a rapid and complete recovery, my dear girl, and I'm sure Mary will join with me in that wish when I tell her the score this evening. We'll be glad to see you back in due course. Keep in touch. Goodbye, Joanna.'

'Goodbye, Richard.' Slowly Joanna replaced the receiver on the bedside phone, a lump in her throat because of Richard's kindly understanding. Now she must show herself worthy of that trust and consideration. She must put the happenings of the last few days behind her and get back into routine as quickly as possible. She must look forward, not back. She had a wonderful job and a boss in a million. Many career women had a failed marriage behind them, she reminded herself. She would join their ranks, and in time the pain would get less. Holding her head high and smiling steadily, Joanna took the lift down to the dining-room, to make herself be sensible and eat some lunch.

The service was friendly and the food no doubt excellent, although Joanna hardly noticed what she was eating and everything was tasteless anyway. She finished off with coffee, the usual strong brew in a tiny cup, and that, at least, she could taste and it was bitter. Still being sensible she returned upstairs to her room and lay on the bed. Resting was the order of things today. Tomorrow life would begin again. A different life because it wouldn't have any hope in it. You had to learn to live without hope.

She had been lying on the bed trying to relax and getting steadily more tense for nearly half an hour when the telephone rang close to her ear. Hal? Her heart stopped beating and she grabbed the receiver and mumbled into it.

'Joanna? This is Rosa. How are you, my dear? Hal's just been here and he's been recounting the story of your horrid accident. I've only just got back from Paris, so I didn't know anything about it. Hal tells me the doctor thinks you should have a check-up in hospital. He's going to be very busy for the next day or two and he asked me if I'd arrange it as I know the ropes in these parts.'

Rosa paused. 'Are you still there, Joanna?'

'Yes, I——' Joanna began, and stopped, Hal had thought about her—had gone to the trouble of asking Rosa to arrange for this check-up. It didn't mean that he cared, of course. It must be merely his sensitive conscience playing up again. Don't read too much into it, Joanna.

'I hope you don't think I'm being interfering, love,' Rosa was saying, 'but Hal was so insistent about it that I've taken the liberty of making an appointment for you for this afternoon. If I call for you at your hotel in about half an hour, could you be ready then? I'm sorry to spring this on you but, as I said, Hal was very emphatic about it. What do you think?'

'Oh yes, I'll be ready,' Joanna said quickly. 'And it's very good of you Rosa, although the hospital will think I'm a fraud—I'm really quite better, except for a few bruises.' A broken heart wouldn't show on the X-ray.

Later that afternoon, as the two women emerged from the hospital and climbed into a taxi, Joanna said, 'There, what did I tell you? No permanent damage.'

Rosa patted her hand as the taxi took them back to Joanna's hotel. 'It's a relief,' she said, 'and it will be a great relief to Hal, I'm sure.'

'Will it?' Joanna said wryly. It didn't make sense that he should be so concerned about her. They had parted and he'd made it plain that no idea of their marriage being revitalised had occurred to him.

Rosa glanced quickly at her, 'Yes, it certainly will.' The soft voice was unusually firm. 'I haven't seen him looking so worried about anything for a long time.' She hesitated as the taxi turned in at the hotel entrance. 'You'd rather not talk about Hal?'

Joanna bit her lip and nodded silently.

They got out of the taxi and Joanna insisted on paying the fare. For a moment they stood together in the forecourt of the hotel, then Rosa said diffidently, 'Would you rather I went, then?' She smiled crookedly. 'Sort of—sever all connection?'

'Oh, Rosa, *no*. Please don't go.' There were tears in Joanna's grey eyes now. 'These two days have been so traumatic and I don't know—I don't understand——' She drew in a quivering breath. 'But please don't think I don't—don't value your friendship. However things are between Hal and me,' she added in a rush.

Rosa squeezed her arm and led the way into the hotel. 'Can you get a decent cup of tea in this establishment?' she said. 'I think we could both do with one.'

When they had given the order and were sitting in comfortable chairs in the lounge, Rosa leaned forward and said, 'Just one more word and then I won't refer to it again. Believe me, Joanna, I know nothing about how things have been, or are, between you and Hal. He's never spoken to me of anything that has happened between you, so don't think I've got any axe to grind, or that I'm trying to act as an intermediary. So now, let's enjoy our tea and later on perhaps we could dine together? It would give me so much pleasure, and I really don't like to think of you spending the evening alone.'

Ever afterwards Joanna was grateful to Rosa for that evening. She knew only too well what would happen if she sat alone in the hotel, or walked alone along the water-front under the palm trees, and she didn't feel equal to discouraging any too-hopeful males that happened to be around. But for Rosa she would have had to spend the evening alone in her room, feeling suicidal.

Rosa was a life-line to sanity. She put herself out to be entertaining and told stories of her life in Menton and the art circle there, and the open-air music festival and the amusing people that gathered for these events, and never once mentioned Hal. She made sure that Joanna ate a good meal at the cheerful small restaurant in a side-street, only a stone's throw from the hotel, and when they finally said good night in the hotel lounge she kissed Joanna and said, 'Now, keep in touch, won't you, Joanna, and don't let it be another two years. And if there's anything I can do to help, in any way at all, you will let me know, won't you?'

Warmed by Rosa's affection and a little hazy with the wine that had kept appearing in her glass at dinner, Joanna promised. And—miracle of miracles—when she finally got into bed she fell asleep almost immediately and slept until the following morning.

Giles was on the phone even before she had dressed. She answered his questions briefly. Yes, she was much better, the hospital had checked her out. She had been in touch with Richard and arranged that she should join Giles in Nice and she proposed to drive over there this afternoon and would be ready to start work immediately.

She could almost see Giles smiling at the other end of the line. 'That's splendid news, I'm glad everything's turned out well in the end.' He meant he was glad that Hal had disappeared from the scene. 'I've got a surprise for you, Joanna, we've been invited to a party tomorrow evening on Weiss's yacht. It's anchored out in the bay— I've been there once and it's quite something, I can tell you. I'm relying on you to come with me and keep the flag of Kilburn Europroperties flying. You never know what this job will lead to. You'll come?'

When he put it like that she could hardly

refuse and a party would fill in the time. The last thing she needed just now was to be alone with her thoughts. But, 'I haven't brought a party dress grand enough for a party on a millionaire's yacht,' she demurred.

'Buy one when you get to Nice,' said Giles grandly. 'I'll come and help you.'

Everything that happened after that had the feeling of an anti-climax. Joanna felt that she was waiting for something—but what was there to wait for? If Hal had meant them to meet again he would have said so or at least given her some hint that he would contact her again. But he hadn't. The fact that he had asked Rosa to keep an eye on her for a while didn't really mean anything, and she couldn't take literally Rosa's remark that Hal was worrying himself sick about her. Joke, she thought, trying in vain to smile. One of the things that had changed about Hal was his habit of turning everything into a joke. She supposed it was his way of avoiding difficult situations.

At least she would be spared the pain of going back to the villa today to pack up the owners' personal belongings. If Hal had leased the villa then she could go inside only with his permission, and she had no intention of seeking that—or of trying to find out from Rosa where she could contact him. The packing would have to be done by someone else at a later date. For her part, the assignment was over.

She found the hired Renault in the hotel car park, as Hal had promised, and collected the keys from the reception desk when she paid her bill and checked out. When she got into the car she found a piece of paper folded round the steering wheel.

'Mind your driving,' Hal had written in a hurried scrawl. 'See you, H.'

What did that mean? Nothing, except that Hal had probably taken a taxi up the hill and driven the Renault down himself, some time when she wasn't in the hotel. He had wanted to make sure the car was there, the car that would take her to Nice, away from him. He wanted to end the little episode as civilly as possible. That 'See you' had been a gesture, not to be taken seriously. They weren't likely to see each other again in the few days that she planned to stay in France. Joanna folded the note carefully and put it in her handbag before she turned the key in the ignition and drove slowly away from the place that held everything that made life worth living.

The following evening was warm and still and the stars that shone down out of a black velvet sky looked huge, reflected in the glass-calm water. Giles placed a possessive arm around Joanna as he lifted her down into the launch that was to take them out to the great white yacht lying at anchor in the bay.

'You're looking very super, Joanna. That dress is definitely a success.'

'Thank you.' Joanna smiled automatically. It seemed that she had lived through the time since she arrived in Nice yesterday as if she were a kind of clockwork toy. She just hoped the clockwork wouldn't run down before the evening was out.

Giles was being very pleasant and he was obviously delighted and flattered with this invitation to mingle with the millionaire set and she wouldn't want to let him down.

'Yes, I think we made a good buy,' he went on with satisfaction as they were helped into padded seats by the uniformed crew-man. 'You should wear red more often. It's very dramatic with your dark hair and pale skin.' He drew in a deep breath of satisfaction as the engine started and the small craft cut its way across the dark waters of the bay.

Joanna herself wouldn't have chosen the scarlet chiffon dress with the glittery trimmings round the low-cut neck. She felt more like wearing black, as if she were in mourning, and the red dress had been hideously expensive. But Giles had waved away her doubts about the price. 'I shall put it on expense account,' he said, with a knowing wink. 'Perfectly legitimate.'

She had her doubts about that but she was beyond caring, or caring about anything else. It would have been nice if she could have felt impressed and thrilled, as Giles was, by the splendour that met them when they climbed aboard the sumptuous yacht a few minutes later. But the atmosphere of luxury and wealth meant nothing to her, and anyway there was nothing new to her about parties given by rich tycoons. She and Hal had been to lots of them when they were together—another young couple who had reached the top.

She allowed Giles to lead her to where a throng

of beautiful people clustered round a bar in a luxurious saloon with small tables and deep velvet lounges, that looked almost large enough to belong to an ocean liner.

'Ah, there's Mr Weiss. Come along and be introduced.' Giles took Joanna's hand and she found herself looking up into the craggy face of the great man himself, the multi-millionaire who could buy hotels and modernise them just for the excitement of it, rather than for profit, for surely he didn't need the money.

'May I introduce my assistant, Miss Joanna Daley, Mr Weiss.' Giles's voice held a calculated tinge of deference.

The big man bowed over Joanna's hand. 'How do you do, Miss Daley? My daughter and I are pleased you could come. This young man has been a great assistance to me with the hotel purchase.' The booming voice spoke perfect English with only a trace of a guttural accent, and Joanna's hand was enclosed in a huge fist. She smiled and murmured the right things and a moment later the big man's attention turned to another of his newly-arrived guests.

Giles procured drinks at the glittering bar and they made their way to a table in a corner. He pulled his chair close to Joanna's. 'Well, what do you think? Some party, eh? I bet you've never seen anything like this before.'

Joanna's eyes moved over the decorative crowd of men and women in their fabulous clothes. It was warm in the saloon and the scent of the massed flowers, mixed with the women's perfumes, cigar smoke and the aroma from dishes of food on the long buffet table was making her head ache. 'Could we go on deck, Giles? It's getting rather——'

Giles wasn't listening. 'Look,' he whispered, his hand closing on hers. 'Over there—the girl in the white dress. That's Denise Weiss—old Weiss's daughter. I've met her once or twice in the hotel. A stunner, isn't she?'

Joanna's eyes followed Giles's and the crowded saloon went out of focus. Only the girl in the daring white satin sheath-dress was clearly, sharply defined, standing in the centre of a circle of admiring males, her luxuriant red hair cascading in a gleaming mass round her bare, smooth, sun-bronzed shoulders. She held a champagne glass in one hand and her other hand rested lightly on the arm of the man beside her. But she wasn't attending to what he said. Her eyes were everywhere, flicking round the saloon, looking for—someone.

Joanna froze inside. Denise. Denise—*Weiss*. The daughter of the man who could give Hal the big contract that meant so much to him! No, she thought. No, no, *no*. Hal wouldn't do that, he wouldn't use the influence of a girl to get him to the top. Or would he? What had he said about the contract, when she asked him? 'It means a lot to me, Jo. It means pretty well everything.'

Giles was chuckling under his breath. 'Daddy's darling daughter,' he murmured, close to Joanna's ear. 'They say she twists the Big Man round her pretty finger, and I shouldn't be surprised if that was true.' Just then Joanna could hear her cry above all the chatter and laughter and clink of glasses. 'Hal—Hal darling, you made it!'

Joanna knew then that this was what she had been expecting and dreading, and she shrank back into her chair like a small animal into its burrow. Hal was standing just inside the door of the saloon, his eyes narrowed quizzically. He wore dark-blue velvet trousers and a white lawn shirt with a lacy frill. His brown, springy hair gleamed under the overhead lights. He looked devastatingly handsome, very much at home, and just a little bored. Denise pushed through the crowd and threw herself eagerly into his arms and held up her glossy lips for a kiss and he bent his head and kissed her lightly and drew away, smiling down into the lovely face raised to him. She linked her hand through his arm and led him to the bar. They stood together with their backs to where Joanna was sitting. Giles had let out a smothered exclamation and his face had turned an ugly red colour. 'Bloody hell,' he muttered through tight lips. 'The clever bastard—so that's what he's been up to. I'll bet you any money Weiss's contract has gone to his firm. Sleep your way to the top, that's the kind of ploy your ex-husband would use, Joanna. You're well rid of him.'

Joanna looked at him.

'Well,' he spluttered. 'It's obvious, isn't it?'

'Is it?' she said icily.

'Look, Joanna, don't be like that. I know he's still your husband but it's over, isn't it, you said

so yourself. And you must know by now the kind
of fellow he is and—and——' The rush of words
hesitated and dried up.

But Joanna wasn't listening. Her eyes were
fixed on the two across the room. Oh God, they
were coming over here. Denise was holding Hal's
hand, pulling her with him through the pack of
guests round the bar, obviously looking for a
secluded table somewhere.

'Well, well, well, look who's here.' Hal's deep
voice set all Joanna's nerves jangling. He had
stopped beside their table. 'Hullo Jo.' His glance
took in Giles with a nod and moved back to
Joanna. 'How are you feeling. Jo? Rosa gave me
the message from the hospital. All OK, was it?
I'm glad.' He looked towards the girl beside him.
'Jo, this is Denise Weiss. Denise—Joanna, my
wife.'

'Hullo, Denise. Lovely party,' murmured
Joanna. The words almost choked her but thank
heaven they sounded quite normal. She saw the
girl's eyes widen and then narrow, and heard her
quick intake of breath. This introduction was a
shock to her but she was a lot tougher than she
looked. She was younger than Joanna had
expected too, much younger than she had seemed
when glimpsed in the car the other evening.
Young and beautiful and very, very rich. And she
twisted her father round her little finger. An
agonising, lacerating thrust of jealousy speared
through Joanna.

'Hi,' said Denise, keeping her hand through
Hal's arm and moving close against him.

She looked towards Giles. 'Hi, Giles, still busy with all Daddy's chores? You should just see Giles's office, Hal.' She laughed up into Hal's face, her glossy lips parted to show perfect white teeth. 'He's a real workaholic, this man.'

Giles laughed immoderately. 'That's better than the other kind any day, Miss Weiss.'

'Oh look, Hal, Daddy's signalling to us.' Denise took Hal's hand and began to urge him back the way they had come from the bar. He glanced over his shoulder towards Joanna and met her eyes with a wry grin that might have been apologetic as he went with Denise to join her father. The three of them stood talking for a moment or two and then left the saloon together.

Joanna watched them go. Giles was still muttering about the contract. 'I'll bet that's what they've gone to talk about. Hell, why didn't I get my hooks into that Denise wench before your blasted husband moved in?'

Joanna felt sick. 'Why didn't you?' she said. A terrible sense of loss was creeping through her, a heaviness that weighed her down. She had to will herself to stand up. 'I need some air, Giles, I'm going on deck. No, don't come with me——' as he reluctantly began to rise '—I'm going to find a loo first. I'll see you later on.' Any excuse to get rid of him, he revolted her.

She walked stiffly up the short companion-way, holding on tight to the brass hand-rail. On deck the air was blessedly cool and she drew in deep, quivering gulps of it. She stood looking round, seeking cover. A small area of the after-deck had been cleared for dancing and a three-piece guitar band was thrumming away softly in a bower of potted shrubs. Garlands of coloured lights swung overhead. One or two couples had come up from below and were moving together dreamily, their arms round each other's necks. Beyond the dancers Denise and her father were sitting with Hal on a slatted wooden seat beside the rail. The two men were leaning together, deep in conversation. Denise was close to Hal, one hand on his thigh, the other arm trailing over the rail.

Joanna turned blindly in the opposite direction, towards the forward part of the boat, out of range of the dancing area. It was dark here, and she leaned over the rail and looked down into the black, gently-moving water, and felt more alone than she had ever felt in her life.

'Hi.' A girl's husky voice made her spin round. Denise Weiss had come up behind her. 'I saw you come along here and I wanted to—just to talk to you for a minute. Do you mind?'

Joanna turned. 'Why should I mind?' It was funny how she could speak in such an ordinary voice. Perhaps murderers felt like this—very calm, very cold.

'Well, I thought—you know—you might resent me.' White hands fluttered in the dim light. 'About Hal and all that. I didn't know you were coming with Giles tonight. It was a bit of a shock meeting you.'

'Yes,' said Joanna. 'What did you want to say to me?'

She heard the girl's tremulous intake of breath. 'Just to say thank you for—for agreeing to a divorce. I was a bit afraid you wouldn't.' She laughed nervously. 'Hal's such a gorgeous man I couldn't believe any girl would let him go, you see.'

Denise was standing with her back to the rail. I'm stronger than she is, Joanna thought, I could push her over the side into the black, heaving water. She closed her eyes; she must be going mad.

'And there's another thing.' The girl sounded timid now, almost apologetic. 'You see—it must sound awful to you—but the fact is that I can do so much to help Hal on in his career—through Daddy, of course. If Hal's in the family there'll be no end to what we can do for him. They're talking now about a big contract that Daddy is giving to Hal—something to do with the Hotel Royale.'

'Yes,' said Joanna again. Everything was becoming clear now. It would all fit in and make sense when she was able to think it out.

'You're such a darling, Joanna, I do hope we can all be friends in a civilised way later on. Thank you, thank you.' Denise leaned forward and a waft of flower-sweet perfume moved in the air. Soft lips brushed Joanna's cheek and she pressed her own lips together in revulsion. Dear God, how much more did she have to take?

'I hope *you'll* be very happy too,' Denise cooed. 'Is it Giles Potter? He's quite a charmer. I think we're both very lucky.'

Joanna put a hand over her eyes. 'Will you excuse me now? I haven't been well and—I'm not feeling too good.' Her limbs had suddenly gone weak and she groped her way backwards and found something—a wooden structure of some kind—to sink down on.

Denise made a soft little sound of sympathy. 'Oh dear, I'm so sorry, and I've been so selfish, worrying you with my problems. You stay here, I'll go and find you a drink to pull you together.' There was a swish of satin as the girl ran back along the deck.

Joanna sat with her head in her hands; she felt terrible. Time elapsed, then suddenly she seemed to be surrounded by people. Hal was there, and Mr Weiss, and Giles, and Denise was hovering in the background.

Hal was holding a glass to her lips and she sipped the brandy and coughed. 'You shouldn't have come tonight, you're not fit.' He spoke at her ear, too low for the others to hear over the twang of the guitars. He sounded angry; she must have embarrassed him by her presence.

'I didn't know,' she muttered.

'You didn't know what?' His voice was urgent, rough.

'Oh—anything,' she said vaguely.

He put a hand round her shoulders and she shrank away. 'Don't touch me,' she whispered.

Giles was there, on her other side. She reached up to him. 'I'd like to go now, Giles,' she said quite clearly and pulled herself up, holding on to his arm. 'Could we go back to the hotel, please?'

Her head was swimming and after that she was only dimly aware of what happened. She knew that the big man himself was taking matters in hand. He was very kind, very authoritative, very concerned as he rapped out orders. A launch was brought alongside, Joanna was somehow bundled into it. Giles had climbed in beside her and they were chugging their way across the dark water.

Back at the hotel Giles took Joanna up to his suite, where she sank weakly into a lounge chair. He moved his shoulders impatiently under his stylish velvet jacket as he stood looking down at her. 'I'll go and find Madame Blissot,' he said, 'she's the housekeeper and she must be somewhere about. She'll know what to do.'

She shook her head. 'Please don't, Giles, I'm feeling better now and I don't want anyone fussing. It was just the heat and the noise. I shouldn't have gone. I'm sorry—I spoiled your evening.'

'*You* didn't,' he said sulkily. 'It was spoilt already, I was glad to get away. It was as I told you, that husband of yours had wangled himself the contract for the electronics. I was pretty cheesed off, I can tell you, when old Weiss broke it to me. He was OK about it, I suppose— brought out a lot of guff about going carefully into all the details before he decided, and he must remind me that my firm had "already negotiated several contacts for him".' He grimaced, imitating the big man's slow, authoritative voice. 'The details my foot! He didn't need to go into the details, he only had to listen to his darling

daughter. Oh——' he spat out an obscene word
'—that kind of thing gets up my nose.'

The mask of the smooth executive had slipped
badly. He swung away and poured himself a
drink at a side table. 'Do you want one?' he said
over his shoulder.

'No,' said Joanna. 'Thank you,' she added.

Giles swung round and threw himself moodily
into the other lounge chair. 'Oh well, I suppose
that's that, I'll have to let my fellows know
tomorrow. Then I'll get on and wind up the rest
of the business here. D'you think you'll be fit to
do some typing for me in the morning, Joanna?'

'I'm sure I shall,' said Joanna. 'I'll go to bed
now and rest.'

Giles nodded absently. 'You do that,' he said,
not looking at her. 'Take an aspirin or something.'

In her own room next to Giles's suite Joanna
sat on the bed and stared at the nearly-full bottle
of aspirins for a long time. But that wouldn't
solve anything if it didn't work, and it would put
a lot of people to a lot of trouble. She swallowed
two tablets, shed the red chiffon dress and left it
lying on the floor as she went into the bathroom
adjoining her room. Coming back, she wrapped
herself in her fleecy gown, because it was warmer
than a nightdress and she was shivering violently.
Then she crawled into bed and lay there staring
dry-eyed into the darkness as the hours dragged
past.

Some time in the early morning she got up and
took two more tablets and after that she slept for

a little time. Breakfast arrived at eight o'clock and
she drank the steaming coffee and left the
croissants and confiture untouched. She had just
finished dressing when Giles knocked and came
in.

'You feeling fit this morning, Joanna?' Giles
seemed to have regained his spirits, he was
looking almost perky again.

Joanna was sitting on the dressing-stool. She
stared at her reflection in the mirror and hardly
recognised the haggard, white face that looked
back at her. 'Yes, thank you,' she said automatically. She would have to react like a robot for
the rest of the time she was here. It might not
be too difficult; she had a feeling that her limbs
were attached to strings and the words that
came out of her mouth were being spoken by
someone else.

The dead feeling persisted all morning.
Automatically Joanna did what was required of
her. Lunch was served in Giles's suite and she ate
the food that was put before her and tasted
nothing. She wore dark glasses to hide the heavy
rings under her eyes.

Giles was being very busy and important and
he seemed to notice nothing wrong with her.
Now that the big contract had fallen through and
he wouldn't be overlooking the work, everything
else would be wound up at the hotel in a day or
two, he told her, and he could move back to his
office and take up the routine work.

'I shall go back to London tomorrow,' Joanna
said and Giles didn't try to dissuade her. She was

well aware that he was disappointed in her, that he thought her a drag. There were so many rich girls around that he could take his pick.

After lunch Joanna said that she would go outside into the hotel grounds. The thought of lying on her bed for the conventional siesta appalled her; she felt that she never wanted to go to bed again. She made her way from Giles's suite down through the great hotel. The alteration work hadn't yet reached the third floor, on which Giles's suite was situated, but below that everything was chaos. The workmen hadn't returned after their midday break and Joanna guessed that they wouldn't return for some considerable time. She picked her way between ladders and buckets and sacks of plaster on the ground floor and stepped over a wet patch where something had been spilled.

Not quite over it, though. Her sandal caught the slippery edge and she began to fall forward, catching hold of a ladder to save herself and letting out a little shriek.

As she straightened up she heard footsteps approaching along the marble floor of the corridor. 'Good lord, Jo, you're not throwing yourself about again surely?' said Hal's laughing voice. 'Where do you think you're going?'

For a moment she just stood staring at him, thankful for the dark glasses that hid her eyes. Then, from a long way away she heard her own voice say, 'What are *you* doing here?' He couldn't be looking for her, could he? *Could he?* No, of course he couldn't.

'I'm on the job,' he said. 'Doing a recce of the premises.'

Of course—stupid of her. Why should he want to see her again?'

'Did you hear that I landed the big contract? Congratulate me, Jo, this means that I'm really on my way up again. I wanted to see you, to tell you about it—you said you'd be pleased if I got the contract.'

'Of course,' she said woodenly. 'You told me how much it means to you and I'm glad you got it.' But I didn't know then just *how* you got it.

He put his arm through hers and led her through a side door into the hotel garden. 'But let's not talk about business, Jo. I came because I wanted to see you—I wanted to know how you are this morning. I was worried about you last night at the party—you looked wretched. As I told you, you should never have gone.'

The blood was returning to Joanna's cheeks now and they were burning. 'It was nothing, really, just the heat and the noise. I'm fine now,' she said.

It was a perfect day, cool for the time of the year. Joanna lifted her face to the cool breeze as they walked along. This had got to be finished as quickly as possible now. No more misunderstandings, no more fantasies about Hal being a changed man who would come and tell her he had loved her all the time and he wanted her back. No more hoping, only to be disappointed. It was finished for good, and all that remained was to take a sharp knife and cut the thread that still bound her to him.

She detached her arm gently from his. 'I'm going back to London tomorrow,' she said. 'But before I go I want to tell you that I'm grateful for what you did for me at the villa. I think I was a little crazy all the time there but I'm myself again now. I quite understand why you thought you had to keep me with you until you'd explained about—about what happened before between us. That's all in the past and, as you said, we can both put it behind us and go on with our separate lives now.'

Beside her Hal had gone very still. She stopped and looked up into his face and it was sterner than she had ever seen it. This final break was infinitely more painful than she had expected, even in her worst moments, but she must go on now.

'I just wanted to say, Hal, that——' she bit her lip '—that I won't contest a divorce and—and I'll wait to hear from your solicitor.' She swallowed hard. 'The sooner the better,' she ended in a rush. She couldn't hide the tears that glinted in her grey eyes. 'I'm sorry,' she faltered, groping for a handkerchief. 'I didn't want to get all worked up, but the end of anything is always a bit—emotional.'

His hands were hanging by his side as he looked away from her, over the wall where pink bougainvillaea rioted. After a long silence he said, 'Is this really how you want it, Jo?' He sounded very tired. This must be a strain for him, too. 'You wouldn't consider trying again?'

She began to tremble. For so long she'd

imagined him saying those words. But not like this—without a word of love—just as if he looked on her as a responsibility that he couldn't shirk. Had she given herself away so dismally when she had begged him to sleep with her up at the villa?

'I don't think that would be a good idea at all,' she said quite steadily. 'Not for either of us.'

His face looked grim in the sunlight. 'As you wish, then,' he said matter-of-factly.

There were steps behind them on the paved path and she looked round to see Giles approaching. He didn't come right up to them but stood apart, saying rather loudly. 'Joanna, I've been looking for you.' He ignored Hal's presence. 'One or two rather important things we need to go over together.'

She smiled brilliantly in his direction. The knife was cutting very clean and sharp now. 'Coming, Giles,' she called back. 'I just stepped out for a breath of air.'

She ran towards him and linked her arm through his. Giles glowered. 'What do you have to talk to that fellow about?' he said peevishly.

'Oh nothing much,' she said. 'Let's go in, shall we?'

She looked back when they reached the door but Hal was nowhere to be seen.

CHAPTER EIGHT

JOANNA had been back in London six weeks before she finally plucked up her courage to go to a doctor. She had registered with a doctor in London a long time ago but had never had to consult one before. It turned out to be a very busy practice and she had to wait over an hour to be seen.

'Yes,' said the young woman doctor briskly, when the examination was over. She was fair and very efficient-looking with huge rimless glasses. At first Joanna had been relieved to find that it was a woman doctor she would be seeing, but now she wasn't so sure.

'No doubt about it, no need to wait for a test.' The doctor looked at Joanna's thin, white face. 'Haven't you left it a bit late to come and see me? You're not married?'

'Yes. Yes, I am,' Joanna said.

'Oh well, no problem then.' The doctor was scribbling on a pad. 'Your husband's happy about the baby?'

'I don't know,' Joanna said wearily. 'I haven't seen him for some time.' She climbed off the couch, pulling on her jumper.

'Oh, like that, is it?' The doctor sat back, pencil poised over the pad. 'Well, how do you feel about it yourself? Have you got a job—will your parents be supportive?'

'I'm sure they will, when they know. They live in the country.'

The doctor nodded, scribbled again, then looked up at Joanna keenly. 'You do want to keep the baby, don't you?'

Hal's child—hers and Hal's. Anger suddenly took over—how dare this woman suggest—— 'Yes, yes, *yes*, of course I do,' she shouted.

'Ssh, my dear, you must keep calm about this.' The doctor's tone had softened a little. 'I have to ask, you know.'

Joanna nodded miserably. 'Yes. I'm sorry.'

The doctor patted her arm. 'This is the address of the clinic then. Go along there as soon as possible. And don't worry—you're lucky to have good, helpful parents. Some girls don't.'

Joanna walked slowly back to her flat across the park. It was a warm June evening; the trees were burgeoning and couples strolled along, entwined, pausing now and again to kiss. Some lay on the grass and Joanna looked away, wincing. When she finally got home she made strong coffee and sat down to phone her parents. She hadn't rung them for over a week, it was difficult to know what to say and it was so awful to have to sound cheery about her trip to France. She didn't know what she was going to say now, probably she wouldn't even tell them at this stage about the baby, but she had to talk to someone.

Her father answered the phone and immediately she knew that something was wrong. 'Joanna—I'm so glad you called. I've been trying to ring you.'

'I've been out most of the evening. Is something wrong, Daddy? You sound——'

'My dear, it's your mother. A minor heart attack early this afternoon. She's in hospital in Wareham.'

'Oh Daddy!' Joanna went icy cold, her own problem forgotten. 'Is it—is she——?'

There was a pause, then her father said slowly, 'I hope and believe she'll be all right, my darling, so you mustn't worry. I wouldn't tell you that if I didn't think it was true, would I?'

'I'll come home,' Joanna said. 'First train in the morning.'

'Oh Joanna, will you? I'd be glad.'

'Of course I will. Will you be seeing Mummy again tonight? Is she conscious? Oh good, well tell her to keep her spirits up and I'll see her tomorrow. And you keep your spirits up, Daddy, I know you'll be a tower of strength to her.'

When she had replaced the receiver she sat staring at it blindly, biting her lip. But Mummy would be all right—Daddy had said it was a minor heart attack, and he was a doctor—he would have known if it was really critical, she comforted herself.

She wanted to rush home now, this instant, but it wouldn't really save time, even if she could get across London in time to catch a night train. She must be calm and sensible and plan. First thing was to let Richard know that she wouldn't be at the office tomorrow. She picked up the phone again and dialled his home number.

Mary Kilburn answered. 'I'm sorry, Joanna,

Richard's out at a golf club get-together. Goodness knows what time he'll be back. Can I help?'

When she had heard Joanna's sombre news she said, 'Oh, my dear child, how worrying for you.' She paused. 'Are you on your own? Yes? Look, I'll hop in the car and come over to you; there might be something I can do.'

Mary Kilburn was a kind soul—a little like Rosa in a way, only Rosa was an artist and Mary was a mother with a family of grown-up girls. Perhaps that was why Joanna, a little while later, somehow found herself pouring out her troubles to Mary as they sat over a late cup of tea in Joanna's living-room.

Mary listened, a small frown gathering between her brows, as Joanna's account of the happenings at the Villa Favorita were disclosed. Finally Joanna sat twisting her fingers together. 'I don't know what to do, Mary. I meant to be weak and go home and unload my troubles on my parents but I can't do that now.'

Mary said slowly, 'Your husband doesn't know about the baby, of course?'

'No—and he mustn't. That would be the end for me, if he thought I'd trapped him. He wants a divorce, Mary, and I promised to give him one straight away. You see—it's rather complicated, but his career will depend on his being free and I couldn't spoil that for him, just when he's making his way up to the top again. And anyway——' she gulped '—it's my own fault that I've got myself pregnant.' She stared down at her hands. 'I made all the running, Mary. I almost begged him to sleep with me that night at the villa. I wanted him back and I thought—Oh God, I'm sorry.' The tears were streaming down her cheeks.

Mary let her cry for a time and when the tears stopped she said quietly, 'All the same, Joanna, I think he should know. You're still his wife, and it's his baby. How do you know he might not want a son—or a daughter?'

'Not by me,' Joanna shook her head and her dark hair fell across her face. 'It's over.'

'But you're still in love with him?' Mary asked gently.

'Yes, more than ever.' The words were muffled. Then Joanna lifted her head and pushed back her hair. 'I'm horribly afraid I'm a one-man woman, Mary. I'm not going to get over it.'

'And of course you want to keep the baby?'

'Yes. Oh, yes.'

Mary was silent for a long time. Then she poured out another cup of tea and said, 'I've got girls of my own, as you know. I'm trying to think what advice I'd give them.'

Joanna wiped her eyes and smiled forlornly. 'They wouldn't be idiotic enough to get themselves into a mess like this.'

'Wouldn't they though? You don't know the half of it, Joanna. I've brought up three of them and I've ceased to be surprised. But my dear girl——' she leaned forward and touched Joanna's arm '——there's really no immediate problem, is there? You must go home to your parents when they need you so badly, and if you're determined not to tell your husband about the baby, then you won't. That will have to sort itself out later. For the moment it's your mother who matters most.'

Joanna nodded. 'You're right of course, Mary. Thank you for coming to my help. I'd got to the stage where I couldn't think sensibly—everything was buzzing round in my head like a swarm of bees. I'll go back home tomorrow morning.'

'Good girl.' Mary Kilburn got to her feet. 'I'll tell Richard—about your mother, he needn't know about anything else for the moment. I hope you'll be able to come back to the office later on—for a time at least. And I do so hope your mother makes a good recovery. Keep in touch and let me know, won't you?'

Once she was at home in the Dorset village by the sea Joanna's own troubles sank into the background. Dr Daley had been over-optimistic about his wife's condition, or perhaps he hadn't wanted to alarm Joanna too badly. For a week her mother was on the danger list and Joanna haunted the hospital, sitting by her mother's bed when she was allowed, holding her hand and trying to will her to live. Caroline Daley had always been so active, so involved in all the good works of the village, it seemed impossible that she should be lying here, helpless, dependent on doctors and nurses and all the life-saving tubes and dials that surrounded her.

'She *is* going to be all right, isn't she?' Joanna pleaded with her doctor father, as she sat at home with him over their evening meal, one ear open or the ringing of the telephone in the hall. 'She eems so—so listless, somehow, as if she'd worn herself out and there wasn't any fight left.'

Dr Daley nodded slowly. 'I know what you mean, Jo. She needs something to get her over he hump. I only wish I could think of something.'

Joanna looked down at her plate. 'Is it my ault, Daddy? I know she must have been upset about my break-up with Hal—do you think it affected her more than she showed? She was such a tower of strength when it happened, I'm afraid I must have been horribly selfish and leaned on her far too much.'

Her father sighed and stood up, pushing back his chair. 'We've all leaned on her far too much, Jo,' he said sadly as he went off to take his evening surgery.

Joanna was driving her mother's car while she was at home, and the following day she arrived at he hospital early. As she sat in the corridor, waiting for permission to go into the small ward in the intensive-care unit, the nurse who was specialling' her mother came out of the ward.

Joanna was on her feet at once. 'Is there any change? Any improvement?'

Dr Daley was well liked in the hospital and, as his daughters Joanna ranked a little higher than most relatives as far as the giving of information was concerned. But the nurse didn't have to speak. Her slight shrug and the sympathy in her face told Joanna what she wanted to know. 'We're doing everything we can.'

'I know,' Joanna said. 'Thank you, nurse.'

The nurse hurried away along the corridor and Joanna sat staring at the shiny pale blue wall opposite. They were doing everything they could for her mother. But she wasn't, there was still something she could do.

Half an hour later she sat beside the bed, holding her mother's hand and talking very softly to the woman who lay so still under the white honeycomb quilt. 'Mummy—I've got some news for you. Wonderful news—I think you'll be glad.'

Caroline Daley's eyelids lifted and a faint smile touched her mouth. 'Good news?' she whispered listlessly. People had been trying so hard to encourage her, to tell her about her garden, about the W.I. and the church garden-party, but none of it seemed to rouse her interest.

'Very good. Listen, darling, how do you feel about being a grandmother?'

She saw the tinge of colour that ran into the greyish cheeks. 'Jo—you're——'

'I'm going to present you with a grandchild, dearest. In about seven months' time.' She waited, watching as her words sunk in.

Then a real smile pulled at her mother's mouth. 'Oh—oh—that's made my day.' The little ordinary expression sounded odd and pathetic, and yet there was a new hint of animation in the tired voice, a new flicker of light in the dull eyes. 'Hal?' came the whispered question.

'We met up again in France,' Jo said firmly.

'And you're——?'

'Going to get together again? Oh, I hope so,

hink everything's going to work out at last.' The
ie came out easily enough.

That afternoon the doctors were almost
urprised to find that Mrs Daley had taken a
lefinite turn for the better. A fortnight later she
vas back home. A long rest would be needed, but
f she took things carefully she would be almost
is good as new.

And three days after that a solicitor's letter
irrived for Joanna, re-addressed from London,
;iving her notice that her husband, Harold James
Randall, was suing for divorce.

The nurse that her father had insisted on
installing to ease Joanna's burden of helping her
mother back to health was attending to the
morning routine up in the bedroom. The
cleaning woman who came in twice a week was
hoovering in the living-room. Her father had left
or his surgery at another of the nearby villages,
leaving his secretary manning the phone in his
office.

At the moment there was nothing for Joanna to
do, no way of busying herself to take her mind off
the official-looking letter that seemed to leer at
her like an obscene threat from the dressing-table
in her bedroom, where she had rushed up to hide
herself when it arrived.

She pushed the letter into a drawer, pulled on
an anorak, because outside there was a drizzle of
rain, and walked down along the lanes to the
beach. It was a long, long stretch of beach, one of
the longest on the south coast. The drizzle of rain
was keeping the holiday-makers away and Joanna

had the beach to herself. The tide was high, almost reaching the sandhills in places.

This was where Joanna had first parted from Hal, when she was a teenager; when he had kissed her and promised to come back some day when he had made his fortune.

This was where, five years later, he had taken the ring from his pocket and put it on her finger and said, 'You see, I came back to claim you, like I promised.'

It seemed fitting now, she thought bleakly, that she should come back here when that romantic fantasy had finally come to its inevitable end.

She walked along the wet sand, watching the waves break sluggishly at her feet. There would be things to be attended to; their own solicitor to see. Her father would help her, she was sure of that. She had had to confide in him almost as soon as she had returned home. It was a painful scene; he had been loving to her and taken her in his arms as if to protect her against the world and against her husband in particular. But he had been deeply angry too.

'Don't feel badly about it, darling,' she had urged. 'Marriages are breaking up all the time you know.'

'I do know,' Dr Daley had said heavily, slumping into his leather chair and looking suddenly so much older that Joanna's heart twisted. 'That doesn't help when your own daughter is involved. It hurts like hell, Joanna, to know that you're hurt. And now—to bring up a baby on your own! I don't know—I really don't know.' He shook his head wearily.

Then he looked up. 'And how will your mother feel when she knows the truth? She believes you and Hal have made it up and that he'll be coming from France any time now, to visit us.'

'I know,' Joanna said bleakly. 'We can't tell her yet.'

Mrs Daley had begun, in the last few days, to enquire about Hal. When was he coming back from France? How soon would Joanna be joining him? Would he be able to spare the time to come to Dorset and visit them?

'It would be so lovely to have a real family party again,' she said wistfully. And Joanna had crossed her fingers behind her back, in a childish gesture of justifying a lie, and promised that they would. But inside she had been weeping silently.

She walked until the drizzle turned to rain, beating rain that stung her cheeks and trickled down the neck of her anorak. This was stupid, it would do no good if she caught a chill, she scolded herself. Making her way across the sandhills to the road she headed briskly for home.

When she opened the front door half an hour later the cleaning woman was hoovering the hall. 'Oh, bless me, Miss Daley, you're soaked. What a morning! And there's someone waiting to see you in there.' She jerked her head towards the living-room.

Joanna groaned. A woman from one of her mother's numerous committees, they called in all the time, and she had never felt less like chatting than she did this morning. No good asking Mrs Brewer who it was—she hadn't lived in the village long and could never remember anyone's name. Perhaps if she went in looking like a drowned kitten Mrs Whoever-it-was would take the hint and depart. She pushed open the living-room door and walked in, a wry smile of apology for her appearance fixed on her mouth.

A tall man turned from where he stood looking out of the rain-streaked window, and her heart gave a great lurch and seemed to stop beating. Hal walked the length of the room to where she stood, transfixed, dripping rain on to the pale-green carpet. 'What do you want?' she whispered.

'You,' he said. 'I can't stand it any longer, you've got to give that Potter fellow his chips and come back to me. Anyway, he wouldn't want to support another chap's baby.'

The room was spinning round. 'How did you know? Oh Hal, you don't have to, just because—it was all my fault—about the baby, I mean—I didn't think about it—but if we could put off the divorce for a few months—so he could have a name——' She began to sob hysterically. 'It's like—like a Victorian melodrama——'

'Shut up, idiot,' he said. 'You've got to get out of those wet clothes, I don't want to have an invalid on my hands again.' He propelled her into the hall, where Mrs Brewer was still vigorously plying the hoover. 'Do you still have the same bedroom?'

As he pushed her up the stairs Joanna was dimly aware of the daily woman standing in the

all with her mouth gaping open and the hoover
booming in protest at being left stationary.

Hal pushed open the door of her bedroom and
closed it with his foot. 'Come on, off with
everything, girl.' With a kind of concentrated
energy he stripped off Joanna's soaking anorak
and the jumper underneath. He sat her on the
bed and pulled off her muddy shoes and the jeans
that were stiff with salt from the sea-water
splashed up by the tide. She made no attempt to
stop him.

'There,' he said finally, when she sat pale-faced
and shivering in bra and lacy pants, her black
hair hanging lank and wet round her shoulders,
her grey eyes dazed and unbelieving. 'Let's get
you into something warm.'

He pulled down a fleecy white bath-robe from
where it hung on the back of the door and
wrapped it round her as she sat on the bed.

'That's better.' He was standing in front of her
staring down at her intensely, and his eyes were
darkly blue and glittering. Then he gave a
smothered groan and pulled her into his arms.

'Jo—darling—sweetheart—you're mine still,
you've got to be.' His kisses were warm and
seeking on her mouth, his hands were warm and
strong as they closed round her body in a
possessive hug. 'You're shivering and you're so
cold.' He lifted his head and looked down at her
sadly and tut-tutted, 'My darling silly child—the
things you do to yourself when I'm not there to
look after you. I think I know a way to warm
you,' he added meaningly.' He put a hand gently

on her stomach. 'Is it OK? Do I still have to be careful with you?' he said wryly.

Joanna's eyes were staring into his incredulously. A miracle was happening and you don't question miracles. Anyway, she was a doctor's daughter and she knew the answer to that one. 'No,' she said and suddenly she smiled. And as she wrapped her arms around him and pressed her body against his, the world had turned the right way up, the blossom on the cherry tree outside her window was dazzling pink, the birds were singing in the rain.

Now—at long last—she had the confidence to ask. 'Do you love me, Hal?'

'*Love you?*' he groaned between kisses. 'I've never stopped loving you for one second of all the dreary seconds we've been apart. And if you don't believe that ask the girls who've done their best to take your place. What a disappointment I must have been to them.' He grinned down at her and she found she could laugh back.

'You might have told me before.'

'No talking now. It's time for action. God, how much I want you.' He was trembling as he shed his clothes and pulled aside the robe that covered Joanna.

The touch of his hands as they roamed her body, finding the sensitive spots so confidently, roused her to a response more passionate than she had ever known before. Intoxicated with happiness, she gave back kiss for kiss, holding back nothing, glorying in the pleasure she was giving as she instinctively moved and touched, and heard Hal's answering groan of rapture.

'I love you—love you——' she cried, and he spoke her name over and over as their lovemaking rose to a climax of passion that left them both shaken and weak and awed. It was as if the separation of the last two years had added a new and deeper dimension to their union.

'Darling sweetheart,' he whispered unsteadily at last, his head pillowed against her soft, swelling breast. 'How could we have ever believed we could stay apart? How could I have been such a bloody fool as to go through the motions of beginning a divorce? But you were so cold and distant when we parted, and when you turned away from me and ran back to Giles Potter I had black murder in my heart.'

Yes, Joanna thought, and I know what *that* feels like. But now wasn't the time to bring up Denise Weiss's name.

'You didn't really want a divorce, did you?' Hal lifted his head and stared down anxiously into her face.

'No,' said Joanna. 'The idea crucified me. I thought you did—I thought that's why you came to the villa—to ask me to forgive and forget, and let you get on with a fresh life. That's what you said.'

He gave a hollow laugh. 'God, what a mess I made of everything. I ought to be awarded a medal for bungling. When I said a fresh life I meant a fresh life—together. But I didn't dare rush you. I thought I had to ease you into the idea. I didn't see how you could still love me after the bloody awful way I treated you. And you kept on saying you were going to marry that oaf, Potter. You never gave me a hint that you still loved me.'

'*Hal!*' Joanna's grey eyes were huge with disbelief. 'How can you say that—when I practically begged you to make love to me?'

He grinned. 'Oh—that! I knew you wanted sex at that moment but I daren't let myself take it for granted that it meant anything more than a passing urge. After what I did to you I reckoned it was going to be a long hard slog to persuade you to come back to me.'

Joanna lay back and stared up at the ceiling. She said thoughtfully, 'Don't you know what they say—that a girl needs to be in love. A man can just enjoy a few minutes' pleasure. Any pretty girl will do.'

He lifted himself and turned her face to him and the tenderness in his own face rocked her to the depths of her being. 'Not true,' he said soberly. 'Not for me. Not any pretty girl—only you, Jo, my dearest love. Without you my world is a desert. And not for a few minutes, I need you beside me for the rest of our lives. Starting now. Yes?'

'Yes, oh yes,' she cried and was cradled warmly, lovingly, against him while the sound of the hoover boomed on below in the hall and the rain hurled itself against the windows.

That day Mrs Daley came downstairs for lunch

for the first time since her illness. She was very thin, and there were new streaks of white in her dark hair, but there was colour in her cheeks again. Dr Daley hadn't returned from his rounds, the nurse had gone off to shop in the town, so there were only the three of them for lunch in the family dining-room overlooking the heath. Joanna had been faintly nervous about the meeting between Hal and her mother. She had never told her parents the details of what had led to the break-up of her marriage, and they had never pried, respecting her silence. But she had often thought that they must have guessed at the cause. Her father, particularly, had been stern and silent when Hal's name had been mentioned at first. Later on, nobody mentioned it at all.

Hal was standing at the bottom of the stairs when Joanna came down with her arm round her mother. He seemed to hesitate uncertainly, waiting, and Mrs Daley moved towards him and held out her arms. 'Hal dear, welcome home,' she said and gave him her lovely warm smile, which was so like Joanna's.

'Thank you, Ma, thank you a million times.' He kissed her and held on to her hands and said quietly, 'You're really better? You've had a bad time.'

'Really better,' she said as the three of them moved into the dining-room. 'You two have provided me with an excellent tonic. And I shall enjoy all the knitting during my enforced convalescence,' she added with a twinkle.

Joanna went into the kitchen to fetch the

shepherd's pie that Mrs Brewer had left in the oven, and when she came back her mother and her husband were chatting away easily as if none of the bad times had ever happened.

'And you're going to settle in France, Hal? That's where your new business is?' Caroline Daley pulled a face at her daughter. 'He's going to take you away again, darling.'

'Not until you're absolutely better, Ma,' Hal assured her. 'Until then I shall be commuting—if you'll have me.' Joanna thought she heard a note of uncertainty in his voice still. This meeting with her parents couldn't have been easy for him.

'*Have* you?'

Mrs Daley's warm smile enveloped the two of them. 'Of course we'll have you, Hal dear, it will be so lovely to see something of you again. It's been much too long.' That was her only reference to the years of separation, but it managed to say more than many words could have done.

Joanna had been listening for the sound of her father's car and as soon as she heard it she was on her feet and running across the gravel as he opened the car door.

'Daddy—Hal's here and—and everything's all right. Oh, do say you're glad.'

Dr Daley stopped dead, frowning, one hand on the car door, and Joanna could only guess at what was going through his mind.

'Please, darling,' she urged.

'Does your mother know?'

'Oh yes, and she's so happy about it. She and Hal are together now making all sorts of plans.'

The doctor put his hands on his daughter's shoulders and looked down at her flushed cheeks and the big grey eyes that sparkled as he hadn't seen them sparkling for a long, long time.'

'And you?' he said. 'But I don't need to ask.' They went into the house arm in arm.

The doctor deposited his bag in the hall and walked straight into the dining-room and Hal was on his feet immediately. Dr Daley kissed his wife. 'Great to see you down for lunch, Caro.' He touched her cheek lovingly and turned to Hal. 'Welcome home, son,' he said and held out his hand.

After lunch the rain cleared away and Joanna and Hal walked along beside the sea, their arms round each other, the breeze blowing in their faces. The sky was blue now, with little white puffy clouds and the sea was ruffled as the waves creamed on to the sand.

'Your parents are grand people,' Hal said. 'Understanding. Tolerant.'

Joanna said, 'I love them very much.'

'I hope our children will feel the same about us,' Hal said and she squeaked, '*Children!* Give me a chance, I haven't produced the first one yet.'

'Oh, we'll have several,' Hal told her complacently. 'It might be nice to have a daughter first—a little girl who'd look like you, my love—and then a son who could carry on the family firm.'

Joanna considered that delightful prospect for a time and then said, 'And what about the family firm? How are things going?' The subject had to be broached some time.

'Swimmingly,' Hal told her, but there was only quiet satisfaction, none of the hectic euphoria with which he used to announce a new triumph in the old days. 'We're going to be busy for some time with the Weiss contract at the Hotel Royale, and that already looks like attracting more business for us.'

'That's good,' Joanna said and added tentatively, 'You have still got the contract with Mr Weiss, then?'

'Still?' Hal stopped and looked down at her. 'What do you mean, *still*? I told you we'd got the contract—that's what I came to the Royale to tell you about—that day before you—left. I had to wait until it was in the bag. After what happened before I told myself that I mustn't rush things. I couldn't ask you to come back to me until I had something to offer you.'

Joanna looked up at him. 'No mink and diamonds?'

'Don't hold it against me, love. I'm a changed man.'

'Are you?' she said, cuddling against him as they walked on into the breeze. People don't change, she thought. Hal would always be ambitious, dynamic, exciting. That was what she had first loved about him. But there was something added now—a new tenderness that turned her heart over when she looked into his eyes. 'I love you,' she said.

'And I love you. God, how I love you.' Hal's voice was shaking.

They walked up the beach to a hollow in the sandhills. The sand was still damp after the rain but they didn't notice as they kissed and held each other close.

'But you didn't answer my question,' Hal said at last, winding a strand of her black hair round his fingers. 'Why did you ask if I *still* had the Weiss contract?'

Joanna fixed her eyes on the tuft of sea-grass that rustled in the breeze. There must be no more holding back, no more misunderstandings.

'Because of—Denise,' she said. She felt his slight jerk of surprise. 'You see,' she rushed on, anxious to get this over, 'I knew you and Denise had—had something going for you. Rosa told me, the first time I saw her, and then, that evening I saw you together in your car and you looked like—like lovers.'

'Jo—I——' he groaned, but she held up a hand to stop him.

'Please, Hal, let me go on. When we met at the villa next day and you said you needed to explain to me and to—to be free to start a new life, I naturally thought it was with her.'

He didn't try to interrupt again but she felt his arm tighten around her. 'I didn't know until that night of the party on the yacht that she was Mr Weiss's daughter, and Giles said that she had a terrific pull with her father and could influence him to give you the contract.'

'And you believed him? Oh lord.' He ran demented fingers through his hair.

She shook her head. 'I didn't believe you would go after the contract that way, however much it meant to you. Then, when I was alone on

the deck Denise came up and—and said she
wanted to thank me for being so reasonable about
agreeing to give you a divorce. She said that her
father could help you so much in your business
when you were one of the family. She seemed so
sincere and genuine. I was green with jealousy
but she made me believe her somehow. You—you
didn't get the contract because of her?' she added
rather timidly.

She thought Hal was going to explode. 'Of
course I bloody didn't. Weiss isn't a man to let
any woman influence his business judgment,
certainly not his daughter, the lying, conniving
little bitch.' His voice rose to a shout and a family
party straggling past with two small children and
a dog stared in their direction.

'And that was why you sent me away the next
day? Was it? *Was it, Jo?* You didn't want a
divorce at all—you didn't want to marry Potter?'
He was shaking her none too gently.

'Of course I didn't,' she said.

'Oh God, if I'd only guessed! But you were so
cool—so remote. You made me feel like a worm
that day in the hotel garden, when you said your
piece. It doesn't suit me to feel like a worm so
later on I began to think, OK, if that's what she
still thinks about me we'd better get on with the
divorce, like she wants.'

'I got the letter from your solicitor this morning,'
Joanna said. 'It was forwarded from London.'

'We'll have a ceremonial burning when we get
back,' Hal promised her, 'and come down and
scatter the ashes in the sea, yes?'

'Oh yes,' Joanna agreed, her eyes sparkling as the bitterness left Hal's voice. 'But what made you change your mind?'

'One thing,' he said soberly, laying his cheek against her smooth black hair. 'I couldn't forget the way we were, back at the villa. I couldn't quite believe that you could respond the way you did unless you were still just a little in love with me. I thought, I must give it just one more try, I must find out if she's really going to marry Potter. So I came back to London and went to look for you in Richard Kilburn's office. He had a client with him but his wife was there and she took me out for a drink until her husband was free. When I'd had several drinks I found myself telling her the odds. She's a very sympathetic lady,' he added.

'I know,' said Joanna softly.

'She just looked at me and said, "Are you in love with her? Because if you are hadn't you better go and tell her so, because she's in love with you, and she needs a father for your baby." When I'd surfaced after that I downed another stiff drink and hugged her and I hope I didn't embarrass her in that pub because it seemed to me she'd saved my life. Then I got on the next train and came down here—and the rest you know.'

They were quiet for a long time and the sun dried the sand and the waving grass, and the gulls squawked over their heads and they clung to each other like two children who have been lost for years and then found each other again.

'Where shall we live?' Joanna said at last, dreamily.

'That's what I've been wondering too,' Hal said. 'All my business is in and around Menton at present, but later on I might start up again in Britain. It depends how things go. It doesn't really matter all that much so long as we're together.'

She grinned up at him, her eyes dancing. 'Hal Randall! I never thought I should hear you say that.'

He rubbed his mouth thoughtfully against her sleek black hair. 'Funny what love does for you.'

He trailed his lips down her cheek and found her mouth again. When they had finished kissing he said, 'Would you care to try the Villa Favorita for a while? I think I've bought it.'

'You *think*?'

He chuckled. 'I haven't been very clear about anything lately, but I remember I signed some papers. A kind of hostage to fortune, you might say. I can only afford one home at the present moment but it might be nice to go back there, if you'd be happy.'

'Happy? What a wonderful idea!' Joanna cried. 'I couldn't think of anything more heavenly. We'd be near Rosa, and Mummy could come and stay when she's better, and the baby could be born at that nice hospital.' She stopped, wide-eyed. 'Hal, I had the strangest feeling when we were there. As if the villa were somehow trying to bring us together again. As if it were pleased to have us back. Is that too fanciful for you?'

He framed her lovely face between his hands and kissed her soft mouth slowly. Then he looked into her eyes and nodded emphatically.

'I believe it,' he said.

Harlequin Presents

Coming Next Month

935 THE IMPOSSIBLE WOMAN Emma Darcy
A landscape gardener has designs on a celebrated Sydney architect. Only he says he isn't interested in a lifetime commitment, and it isn't in her nature to settle for less.

936 LONG JOURNEY BACK Robyn Donald
The man she loved jilted her in favor of a more advantageous marriage. Now he wants her back. But why should she trust him just because he's divorced and says he never stopped loving her?

937 PRISONER Vanessa James
The daughter of a wealthy businessman appears to be the target of an elaborate kidnapping in Rome. Why, then, is the kidnapper so determined to hold the young girl's companion—if it's money he's after?

938 ESCAPE FROM THE HAREM Mary Lyons
Four years ago an estranged wife was lucky to escape the desert kingdom of Dhoman with a broken heart. Now her heart is on the line when her husband, the new sultan, demands her return—with their daughter.

939 GLASS SLIPPERS AND UNICORNS Carole Mortimer
An easily flustered secretary succumbs to pressure when her quick-witted boss persuades her to pose as his lover to help flush out the saboteur of his business holdings in Florida.

940 THE LONELY SEASON Susan Napier
On an island near Fiji, the man who accused a children's book illustrator of destroying his sister's marriage needs her help to win the love of his deaf son. It's her chance to prove her innocence at last.

941 WIN OR LOSE Kay Thorpe
Desire was never the problem in the troubled marriage between a journalist and a famous sportsman. Communication was. No wonder her husband refuses to believe divorce will solve everything.

942 SHADOW PRINCESS Sophie Weston
A Paris research chemist can't understand her aristocratic cousin's unwise love affairs—until a certain concert pianist makes her feel alive—almost reckless—for the first time in her life.

Available in December wherever paperback books are sold, or through Harlequin Reader Service:

In the U.S.
P.O. Box 1397
Buffalo, N.Y.
14240-1397

In Canada
P.O. Box 603
Fort Erie, Ontario
L2A 9Z9

ATTRACTIVE, SPACE SAVING BOOK RACK

Display your most prized novels on this handsome and sturdy book rack. The hand-rubbed walnut finish will blend into your library decor with quiet elegance, providing a practical organizer for your favorite hard-or soft-covered books.

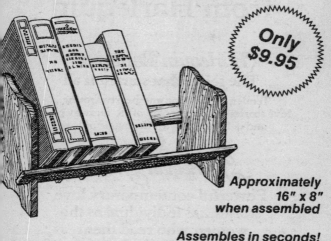

Only $9.95

Approximately 16" x 8" when assembled

Assembles in seconds!

To order, rush your name, address and zip code, along with a check or money order for $10.70 ($9.95 plus 75¢ postage and handling) (New York residents add appropriate sales tax), payable to *Harlequin Reader Service* to:

In the U.S.

Harlequin Reader Service
Book Rack Offer
901 Fuhrmann Blvd.
P.O. Box 1325
Buffalo, NY 14269-1325

Offer not available in Canada.

BKR-1

Six exciting series for you every month... from Harlequin

Harlequin Romance·
The series that started it all

Tender, captivating and heartwarming...
love stories that sweep you off to faraway places
and delight you with the magic of love.

◆

Harlequin Presents·

Powerful contemporary love stories...as individual as the women who read them

The No. 1 romance series...
exciting love stories for you, the woman of today...
a rare blend of passion and dramatic realism.

◆

Harlequin Superromance®
It's more than romance...
it's Harlequin Superromance

A sophisticated, contemporary romance-fiction
series, providing you with a longer,
more involving read...a richer mix of complex plots,
realism and adventure.

Harlequin
American Romance™
Harlequin celebrates the
American woman...

...by offering you romance stories written
about American women, by American women
for American women. This series offers you
contemporary romances uniquely North American
in flavor and appeal.

◆

Harlequin Temptation™
Passionate stories for
today's woman

An exciting series of sensual, mature stories of
love...dilemmas, choices, resolutions...
all contemporary issues dealt with in a true-to-life
fashion by some of your favorite authors.

◆

Harlequin Intrigue
Because romance can be quite
an adventure

Harlequin Intrigue, an innovative series that
blends the romance you expect...
with the unexpected. Each story has an added
element of intrigue that provides a new twist to
the Harlequin tradition of romance excellence.

Harlequin Books·

PROD-A-2

Take 4 novels and a surprise gift FREE

FREE BOOKS/GIFT COUPON

Mail to **Harlequin Reader Service®**

In the U.S.
901 Fuhrmann Blvd.
P.O. Box 1394
Buffalo, N.Y. 14240-1394

In Canada
P.O. Box 609
Fort Erie, Ontario
L2A 9Z9

YES! Please send me 4 free Harlequin Presents® novels and my free surprise gift. Then send me 8 brand-new novels every month as they come off the presses. Bill me at the low price of $1.75 each ($1.95 in Canada)—an 11% saving off the retail price. There are no shipping, handling or other hidden costs. There is no minimum number of books I must purchase. I can always return a shipment and cancel at any time. Even if I never buy another book from Harlequin, the 4 free novels and the surprise gift are mine to keep forever.

106-BPP-BP6F

Name	(PLEASE PRINT)
Address	Apt. No.
City	State/Prov.	Zip/Postal Code

This offer is limited to one order per household and not valid to present subscribers. Price is subject to change.

ILP-SUB-1RR